Janet +
love, sweet
more to come,

Surf Over Sand

Maggie

xxx

Surf Over Sand

Maggie M. Grimshaw

Kennedy & Boyd

Kennedy & Boyd
an imprint of
Zeticula Ltd
The Roan
Kilkerran
KA19 8LS
Scotland.

http://www.kennedyandboyd.co.uk
admin@kennedyandboyd.co.uk

First published in 2014
Copyright © Margaret M. Grimshaw 2014

Cover design © Cats Solutions (cats-solutions.co.uk) 2014

ISBN-13 978-1-84921-142-0

To the three men in my life
Angelo, Joshua and Paul

Acknowledgements

A huge thanks to Paul, my wonderful, caring husband of almost 40 years for the birthday gift which led me on this new road with new goals.

Thanks to Serge, Agnes and Cleve. I would not have had some important threads to this story without having had the good fortune to cross your paths.

To Elaine Branch, Jacqui Brown, Dot Haken, Marietta Huffer, Anne Kirby, Jackie Longbottom, Toni O'Donnell, Margaret Pedley, Steve Alexander Smith, Judith Syzszlo, and Gillian White, your input, encouragement and support throughout this adventure is so very much appreciated.

ONE

An apartment balcony on the edge of a small seaside town in south-east England. Seated there is a pretty, blonde woman who must be in her mid-thirties. A woman lost in deep reverie whose gaze is fixed far beyond those balcony railings. On closer examination, Lydia McIntyre looks slightly dishevelled; her face is streaked with tear stains. In front of her there is an empty seaside promenade. Directly below her, at the foot of her apartment block, there lies a pretty garden laid out with neat lawns. Bronze plaques dedicated to past souls and graffiti dedicated to present ones adorn the benches. Flower beds are blooming with swaying daffodils and hyacinths. This is such a quiet spot, away from the town, with its tired, peeling shopping precinct and traffic noise. It is so secret and private now that all those former seaside visitors prefer to hop on a plane and walk along foreign promenades.

An old black poodle comes into view, pulling an arthritic head-scarfed lady along. As she walks, the little lady's bowed frame sways from side to side. The two of them interrupt Lydia McIntyre's thought pattern. Lydia looks beyond them towards the sea.

Lydia looks out on the scene from that balcony in the south-east of England on a balmy day in April. There is a sudden gust of wind and a large white bundle shoots by right in front of her. A discarded bag of washing comes to her mind in the split second as she sees the object go by. Spilling out of its bag, flailing and flapping, what did she see, too late, passing by, passed by, falling, falling, fallen. A dull thump. Three seconds have elapsed. What does Lydia do? Peer over the balcony? Look above?

*

Did I see hair, yes, dark hair, long dark hair... and do I scream? No, I sit and say to myself, this never happened, this is what I just thought, not what I just saw. I remain still, totally rigid. My body aches. Until the wailing of sirens brings me back to the balcony, back to bald reality. I stare and stare. At nothing in particular. The bell on my door is buzzing. Finally I stand wearily, unsteady at first, and make my way towards it.

"Could you just go over the events again, Madam?"
The detective wants me to describe a scene which had lasted but a mere few seconds, how am I to explain anything more? I am by now brutally aware that I have been witness to more than just a dropped bag of washing.
"Think carefully, you may not think it important at all, but the slightest information could help us. Just let your mind retrace the moments. We have to try and piece this together. Take your time. For example, can you recall hearing anything prior to the incident?"
I struggle to haul myself back in time, to the instant before that bundle goes hurtling by. At that precise moment, I am looking out to sea, contemplating not the clouds scudding across the April sky, nor that little old lady and the poodle taking her for a walk. I am planning murder. I am making a monumental decision. Ending my husband's life without incriminating my own has overtaken my subconscious. Calm, but nevertheless decided, I have to find a way to break free. I owe it to myself. I have been too long downtrodden and bullied. Today, I have reached a point of no return. I am becoming more and more assertive as I think on my balcony. If I were to leave him, he would find

me. If I sued for divorce, he would fight me. But if I were to kill him, I risk only being found out. The third eventuality of being discovered wouldn't bring him back either. He would still be in the world of "was", not "is". But this is to be a master plan. I will not be a suspect. And I will succeed. I am starting to feel that I can do this. I can restart my life. I don't have to just put up with it any more. It is at this point that there is this interruption.

I learn from the police officer that the horrible dull thump was a young woman. The woman who had recently moved into the upstairs flat and whom I had not yet met. Now I never would.

Over fifteen years of marriage to this man have turned me into a person whose feelings are never shown. I am true to my inner voice, but not to others around me. How would the policeman react if he knew that the reason I cannot remember anything prior to the incident is because this bundle toppling past me was no event for me? True, it shocked me somewhat. But I was thinking so hard, so very hard. I was planning to rid myself of Douglas, feverishly planning to escape from my childless, empty marriage to this man.

I must try not to think about that now. I must concentrate on the question. I can feel the policeman looking at me, curious to know something. The silence between us is long and heavy, yet still I do not speak. In a way, this whole episode is becoming a singular irritation to me. I cannot think about my plan now. I have to answer him. I can feel him staring at me, almost into me; maybe he is feeling sorry for me, perhaps he is willing me to open my mouth? Yet no words can come out, I look beyond him, beyond the table, beyond the window, beyond my balcony, back to the view of the sea wall and the waves curling inexorably over it.

A series of stinging blows to the side of my head, there where no-one could see the bruising, or if they did happen to spot it, would never suspect that it came from Douglas's hand laying blow after blow on it. Beaming, jovial Douglas whose hand is his weapon. He had stormed out, and there I was, on the balcony, hoping he would crash the car and die, hoping and praying as I hoped each time he went out after one of these beatings.

Not one single person would ever suspect that he is violent towards me. People might talk of his drinking because he does have a reputation for enjoying a tipple. But they will say that it is nothing to be concerned about among his many qualities; I can hear them saying it. Doubtless they feel it has something to do with me not giving him what he needs, but how many people harbour secrets? How many women or men live with deep, deep hatred of their partners like I do? Am I the one who should accept or am I the victim? I think I am like a multitude of others, submissive, subdued, subjected, accepting that this life is normal, when the only thing that is normal around me is me. Is it normal for someone to strike blows because that person can be sure that the other will not strike back?

At the weekends he generally starts drinking at around 10am. He comes back from the Golf Club and pours himself a whisky. By 12.30 he has drunk half a bottle, and the argumentative, alcohol-fuelled behaviour usually begins over lunch. I become the hunted one. Douglas is good-humoured with others and full of bonhomie. He only ever drinks to excess behind closed doors. And I am loyal, too humiliated to be otherwise. But loyalty turns into dark loathing, when time after time it is tested. Each time after storming out and leaving me in a heap of smudged tears, untidy hair and bruises, Douglas returns abashed, full of excuses, holding a box of exquisite lingerie, or a couple of tickets to the opera. And I accept, time after time, year after year, I accept. My mother, like all the others, knows nothing of this terrible secret. She worships my husband and she never ceases to remind me how lucky I am. How lucky am I?

It is amazing how forgiving I have been, how I can always see the good, not the vileness. How I can always think that

4

that time is the last time, that from now on, things will be different. It is uncomplicated and less irksome to the soul to manage shame and pain when one thinks that they will never return. Putting them on that highest bookshelf of misery out of reach of one's thoughts, I can almost forget they exist. Until the next time, when they surge out and envelop my being once more.

But even someone as ashamed as myself, as desperate to make things work, reverts one day to finding a way to attack. An animal who is taunted and pushed into a corner will eventually retaliate. Something in the head, the bruised and battered head, snaps. And that happens today. Like the tortured bull in the arena, there is an occasional matador, or picador whom that poor beast vents his fury on. An eye for an eye and all that. I make up my mind in an instant and know I will do it. Now I have to plan with care and precision. The preparation is under way when it thunders past. Douglas McIntyre has been spared, at least for a while.

"Take your time, there's no rush. Would you like us to try and call your husband now?" asks the portly detective, in gentle tones, talking to me like an older brother might talk, protecting, caring. Not what one tends to expect of the police after all those TV series.

I have already said he's out in the car. Here am I, actually defending him. Imagine them calling him and him coming down to the police station, reeking of alcohol. All this is to do with shame, in fact. I live a complete lie of a life.

"Thank you, officer. I think it would worry him unduly and he might have an accident driving here." If only, if only. So I eventually step out of my world and try to remember what was going on around me. I struggle and frown and the detective looks on hopefully, but the only thing that is clear is the decision I have made.

"I am ever so sorry, officer, I just can't think of a single thing. It all happened so quickly, it is such a shock. I just saw something go past. Until the police arrived and said it was a young girl who had fallen, I had no idea, none. I heard nothing at all. This must sound very lame, it is as if it was all a dream now. I did see the hair, dark hair, long dark hair and there were things flapping, but I can't say whether it was arms or legs or hair... and there was a white sheet or a towel."

The horror of it had not struck me until that moment.

"A white towelling bathrobe, Madam. Our liaison unit will be contacting you later on just in case. You never know, and of course, if anything comes to mind, just give me a call. This is my direct line number."

He handed me a card, and touched my arm gently, as I stood up.

"It's been a terrible day for you. You must try and get some rest. We've arranged for a car to take you home. Are you sure you don't want me to phone your husband now?"

I thanked Detective Inspector Boswell but politely refused. I stepped into the police car and all the way home I still only thought of nothing but how to rid myself of Douglas. It was as if this event had somehow or other strengthened my willpower, made me into the person I needed to be. That girl had fallen, and here I was, planning my freedom. I was in the safety of a police car. I opened the front door of the flat, turned and thanked the young policewoman who had driven me home.

No Douglas to greet me with flowers or a gift. I breathe more easily, go forward to the balcony doors and stand there behind them, thinking of myself sitting out there this afternoon. A peaceful place where I had been thinking the darkest of thoughts as I became witness to an attempted suicide. As that most dreadful of thoughts passes through my mind, I realise that I have not even asked if she did survive.

The same policewoman came back, two hours after dropping me off. As I opened the door, for a brief clear moment, I brought to mind the scuffling and harsh sounds I had heard before I saw the bundle fly past the window.

6

It was so clear now, that I was shocked not to have remembered it at the police station. It was as if seeing the policewoman there in front of me had cleared the film of forgetfulness from my mind. I was about to tell her when she held up a hand. Behind her stood a young, very young policeman. He looked at me then down at his feet like a punished schoolboy.

"Mrs McIntyre, could we come in? I am afraid I have some bad news..."

At roughly the same moment that the kind, fraternal D.I. Boswell had tried to persuade me to make a phone call to him, Douglas and Douglas's car had slammed into a wall at 50 mph.

Douglas has been transferred to intensive care. Would I come to the hospital, do I want to phone a relative, do I need help to pack a few things for myself? Questions flood over me like surf over sand, sinking in and leaving no trace; I stand mute and disbelieving at the door. They have asked to come in but I have not moved. Slowly I return into their world and back away from them down the hallway. They follow. As if in some bizarre tango movement. All that is needed is the plucking guitar and the clicking of heels. With my first words since opening the door an aeon before, I ask the most dim-witted of questions, yet it is so pertinent. No they don't know whether he will survive. For the second time in my life, the second in that very day, I find myself in a police car, this time being driven to hospital. The first and last time I was in their car, I was dreaming of a life alone. He has snuffed out my right to think for myself. Now I am going to see his broken body. People in this situation must pray for time to wind back, for the accident never to have happened, for today to be yesterday. But how many people go through this kind of situation praying for death not life? How many of them vow to start life if this one is ended, promising self-redemption if only, if only...

"The first 24 hours are crucial. He has sustained many internal injuries but the angle at which the car hit the wall was the main reason why he was not killed instantly. It would appear that he swerved at the last second. We need to complete further tests to ascertain what brain injury he has sustained. From what we have seen on the X-rays, it appears that there will be some damage, but we will have to wait for the results of the scan. The surgeon on call today will look at the scan, then it will be up to him to make a decision whether to operate or not. In this kind of situation, I advise the patient's close relatives to take it an hour at a time. I see that you are alone. You really need to think of informing someone else, someone from your husband's family perhaps. Then you can share this and get some support. From here, we can give you the phone number of a social worker and the voluntary helpers at the hospital will give you all the assistance they can. They are listening ear you know, time to gather your thoughts together and help you try to move through this ordeal."

"Thank you, Doctor," I say mechanically.

There is no proper family of any sort to ring. My own family, like my marriage, is a small, pathetic affair. My parents divorced many years back. My father is a sculptor, living in the Canaries with a Tunisian girl a third his age. Pathetic is the right word. Laurence Waterman is a former father. He has re-started his life. I am part of his other one, I have no particular feelings about him at all. I haven't seen him for a very long time, in fact, since ... my wedding day.

Douglas and I are childless; four miscarriages have put paid to that. I am 35, Douglas 52. He decreed adoption as a no-no a few years ago. With the same violence of his hand and fist, he has withdrawn my right to think for myself, to have an opinion on that subject. I will not be a mother. Douglas speaks in the plural on many subjects and I agree. I exist through him, in fact I am his child. Why would he want another?

My story is that simple romantic tale of teenage girl meets man, not boy. I married Douglas when I was 19, at the end of my second year at university and he an education lecturer of 36. I met him in the university gardens and he took over my life from the moment I saw him. I fell in love with the clever, witty, wildly handsome Douglas; I fell in love with the idea of truly loving someone. Mother adored him from the start, decreed he was the perfect match. I had actually managed to please her. With the marriage she was relieved of some financial pressures. She had, after all, brought my younger brother and myself up over those last four years single-handedly. She had gone back to work as a librarian full-time to pay us through school and college. We had never really wanted for anything. She reminded us every day of that.

Douglas was the dashing bachelor with the seafront apartment and the flashy sports car. The stuff of fairy tales; and he needed a wife as his next asset. We were married in church after a heady courtship through that second year at university. During the summer, when all my friends were taking off for their gap years across the globe, I chose the frothy lace gown, the flowers and ribbons on the pews. And the mother of this bride, a certain Mrs Jane Waterman, resplendent in designer hat and gloves, stoically jovial with everyone despite the awkwardness of Father being there. She had barely concealed her fury as the day progressed. There was the lady soprano hired through Mother's Bridge Club contacts, who belted out *Ave Maria* and *Jerusalem* to Mother's immense pride.

Father, home from the Canaries for the first time since he had walked out on our family four years earlier. There to give me away, as if he had never left. There is an oddness about that term, "giving away". Father could not give me away as he did not possess me. However, he performed the duty and I could tell he was proud to do it. And I was happy to see him once again. Children are not hidebound by expectations. I was certainly still a child on my wedding day.

My little brother, Anthony, was the gawky teenager, who spent the day and evening sulking as 15-year-olds do. I was in tulle heaven, Douglas was my Superman, there I was Lois Lane, being transported through the skies of happiness. I, Lydia Susan Waterman, became Mrs Lydia Susan McIntyre and perfect bliss began. That profound happiness lasted for two years. Until just before my 21st birthday, when I had my first unplanned pregnancy, and my first miscarriage. Douglas's fury when I announced that I was pregnant was only equalled by his evident pleasure when I lost the baby two months later. I began to realise that Superman was a cartoon hero. Douglas's temper was uncontrollable around me, yet largely invisible to the outside world. I had started to fall out of love and into fear.

I began to realize too that I was trapped in the marriage. I was afraid of him, and alone with that fear. I was unable to share my feelings with anyone. I soon learned how to keep the peace, by being totally submissive, never contradicting him, always trying to please him. After a time, I realised that this life was simpler than running the risk of arousing his anger. Douglas wasn't all bad. He was popular in company and people looked on us as the couple they admired. I started to re-invent myself around his moods, trying to please him. I was particularly careful never to complain.

I completed my course in landscape architecture as a married woman and started a job in an architect's office in Cambridge. Douglas worked part-time at the university as well as teaching in a Cambridge primary school. He became Headteacher of the local primary school six years ago.

He decided that we should start a family after my promotion in the company. I was starting to be sent off on assignments here and there; I didn't think that mattered to him. My particular speciality was urban redesign. I was involved in projects which were recreating the urban renewal areas of the Thatcher era. Whenever I returned from an assignment, he was so loving, there were flowers on the table, chocolates on the pillow, and torrid lovemaking.

When I was promoted to the post of assistant landscape designer in the company, Douglas decided we should make a second baby. He persuaded me to leave the job, to prepare for a family, given my first miscarriage. He put that down to working. The company offered me some part-time work at home, which was a side step in my career but meant I could carry on doing some professional work. More than that, it kept Douglas reasonably happy. So I resigned, and thus followed three more miscarriages, four disappointments, four dead babies. In between each there was the poking and prodding, the hospital stays, the tests, the scans, the operations, the hormones, the charts, the lovemaking to order when I was likely to conceive. At the news of achievement at conceiving there was the wonderful euphoria of pregnancy swiftly and sadly succeeded by the profound sorrow of bereavement.

After each dead baby, there came a further change for the worse in Douglas. Drinking fuelled his free time in the apartment. He became more involved in the Golf Club. His appointment as Head of the local school saw his pupils become his children. He continued his work as a visiting lecturer. He was revered as a Headteacher, respected by all and feared by me. Never was there mention of my returning to work, and my confidence in myself had been sapped. My part-time work continued but as time went by I no longer felt able to assume anything other than my role as his wife. My former boss soon tired of my excuses and stopped calling me. The role of housewife was all I devoted myself too, lurching from one weekend to the next, when his drinking bouts were more frequent and when I had to be more and more careful, in order to avoid wreaking his wrath.

My family is small but Douglas's is even smaller. His father is dead. His mother and father came to our wedding, immensely proud of their youngest child and only son. Mr McIntyre senior died of a heart attack three weeks later. Douglas's mother, a tiny bird-like lady of 82, is in a care home in Leicester, now suffering from Alzheimer's. She has returned to her childhood, locked into a world of yesteryear, knowing no-one, other then the faded photographs of her own mother and father. Douglas has an older sister, Heather, who lives in New Zealand. She sends the odd e-mail and the regulation birthday and Christmas card but no more, and neither does he. I do not to contact her either. This is one of the few things I have control over.

My mother lives close by and adores two people ... herself and Douglas, in that order. Of course, how fortunate I am to have him, how privileged to be married to a man who cares so deeply for me. How would any other man accept so selflessly the fact that his wife couldn't give him children? Am I now ready to phone her and tell her that her beloved son-in-law is lying between life and death? No, not yet, at any rate. Do I want her there to see me dry-eyed, dry-mouthed, in rapt expectancy of a sympathetic doctor telling me I am free?

That sulky teenager at my wedding, my younger brother Anthony, works in Singapore for a food company. He has only met Douglas a few times and Mother feeds him stories of how wonderful our life is together, how very privileged Lydia is to have such a wonderful husband. I haven't been able to talk to Anthony about how I feel since I was seven and he was three. I do not know Anthony.

I do the obvious thing. Nothing. I sit there, minutes, hours, days, I have no idea how long I sit there in that sterile hospital corridor. And what of my mother's cherished son-in-law, Douglas, my despised Douglas, what of him? The surgeon has seen the scan. His assistant has explained that they need to ease pressure on Douglas's brain, caused by a blood clot. They are operating now. But I am not thinking of all that; I am miles away, on my own, regaining my life in my thoughts. I am jerked out of my trance by a movement in the corridor. I look up.The surgeon comes along the corridor, slowly taking off his protective cap, smoothing his hair. He removes his gloves in a deft twist, locking one into the other in a small ball.

"Mrs McIntyre, my name is James Philpott. I have just operated on your husband and removed a blood clot from the left hemisphere of his brain. It is very early days yet as we aren't sure if there are other lesions but he is a very lucky man as we were able to operate quickly. Pressure building up in the brain before the operation would have caused permanent damage. He has a chance of making a good recovery. The next 48 hours are crucial. He has been placed in an artificial coma so as not to put his other organs under any stress. It is a normal procedure with head injuries of this nature. He will need your full support and the support of his family. He has various other internal injuries which we are monitoring closely. We are as yet unsure as to whether he will need further surgery. The orthopaedic man will need to see him once he is out of the artificial coma. But you can breathe a tiny little bit easier now. Incidentally, it's maybe not the right moment for this, but we have met before, a couple of years back. My wife and I were at the same dinner table with you both at Kings Golf Club."

I tried to think of all he had just said, did I know him, had I seen him before, did I know his wife? I gazed ahead and murmured a thank you, without replying. He placed a reassuring hand on my shoulder and told me he would see me again over the next few days.

I reflected on the day's events and thought briefly of what had started off this terrible afternoon. My mind went back to the incident which had sent Douglas into a fury. After an uneventful morning, cleaning, ironing, preparing lunch, deciding what to wear for the Rotary Dinner the following Saturday, I had spilled some soup. Just that. The feeble error, the tiny mistake that had set off the chain of events. No, no, the error was not mine, the error was his drinking. That was what this was all about. Had they breath-tested him, I wondered? Where had he crashed? But what difference did it make now anyway?

Once Mr Philpott had left me, I dutifully rang my mother leaving a message telling her I was going home for the night. She would not approve of my leaving him. She would call it desertion. She approved of little of what I did. She didn't even know what had happened that afternoon on the balcony. Her preoccupation with Douglas had filled all her conversation when she had arrived at the hospital earlier and as usual she left me no opportunity to tell her anything. She had stormed up to me, berated me again for not having contacted her.

"Lydia, oh Lydia, why didn't you ring? This is just typical of you. You have always been so secretive. I don't deserve it, you know. No-one deserves to be treated like that, least of all your own mother. How could you not let me know? Don't you realize how hurt I am? Do you only ever think of yourself? Just imagine the shock I got when Mrs Marsden came to the door and told me her daughter-in-law had come home from Ely and had seen Douglas's car being towed away! Of course Lisa rang her husband to check and he being in the ambulance service, he got the information first hand and rang his mother to tell her. Then I got on the phone and tried you, then I tried your mobile, and you know how I never ring you on that thing, it's so expensive ..."

Jane Waterman had prattled on and on. She had sobbed and sobbed loudly then suddenly announced that she was leaving, that she just couldn't bear the strain. She turned as she was pushing open the swing doors and called out to me, "I need to take my mind off things, I have to get ready for my Bridge Club dinner". I had the distinct feeling that she was in such a state of shock that she really couldn't see how crassly selfish she was being. I knew quite plainly that she didn't want to stay because I was there. She didn't want to have to console me; she had never been able to do that. The only friendly, loving arms that I remembered around me were those of my errant father. He was the one to tend my grazed knees and kiss me goodnight. He had left us so suddenly and without explanation that I had wondered long and hard what had happened. Mother had tearfully explained that we were a threesome now. At 15 I was only interested in make-up and magazines but even so I still missed my father's attention and his embraces.

Mother had, for as long as I could remember, been in a bad temper when I was around. As she turned away she had pointed back at me and said that she would be back. Perish the thought, I mused. The early evening had passed and I had stayed alone. I had scrutinised the corridor and its shiny marble-effect floor with scuff marks. Every time the swing doors on either side of me squished open I lifted my head and looked blankly at the faceless people coming toward me. Nurses, visitors, porters, all with their own reasons for being in this place; they often smiled as is the custom. Finally, after an interminable wait, the surgeon had come along. He was warm and friendly. I had listened to him without really hearing. He had left me with a warm smile and he had touched my personal space with a reassuring hand. It had not been unpleasant to feel that someone cared a little. Suddenly I felt worn out. I held my head and noticed how sore it felt. That reminded me of all that had happened in the five or so hours since I had once again suffered a beating.

As I walked into the apartment, I rang the police station back. Yes I had remembered something, yes I would come down to the station tomorrow, yes I would appreciate a car. Yet another police car.

That night I dreamed of islands and sunshine, of times past when life was sweet, of blissful walks along deserted beaches, of sunsets and ochre skies. Of being alone. And when I awoke, I felt strangely rested, tranquil. I laid there alone, for the first time in many years, alone, happy, at peace. I had not thought of Douglas at all ... or the girl upstairs.

The phone rang shortly after I had woken and once more I became the witness.

"Mrs McIntyre? You said you would you be able to come down to the station? Right ho, I'll have a car sent round for you. Thank you so much."

"Just relate what you remember, Mrs McIntyre, take your time, no rush."

"I had been sitting out on the balcony for a good few minutes. I had been in the bathroom before that. During the time I was on the balcony I was just daydreaming so I can't remember so clearly. Then just before the incident, (I was unable to call 'the girl falling' anything other than that) I seem to think that at the back of my mind, there were other noises, which somehow or other registered with me. There were low murmurs, louder tones, then a thudding, a desperate thudding, some scuffling and the bundle crashing past, so near to me. I don't even know if she survived."

And my voice trailed off ... but I knew then that she had been so near that if I had cared to reach out I could have touched her.

"I have to tell you that she did not survive. Thank you Mrs McIntyre. Your husband's accident must make this statement even more difficult for you, but I do need to ask you a few questions. Can you tell me at what time he left the apartment?"

"About 1.30pm. He didn't finish his lunch."

"Could you tell me why he left so abruptly?"

"We had a little difference of opinion during our meal and he got up and left, rather than continue the argument. He often does that, then he drives around for two or three hours and when he comes back, we both apologize. Only this time, he didn't come back."

I sobbed bitterly, uncontrollably. To the mere observer, I was the shocked young wife in distress. I had witnessed an horrific accident and my husband was lying in intensive care. I will not shout aloud to that same society that this man is the vicious wolf in sheep's clothing. I do care about what others think.

"Mrs McIntyre, you have undergone two shocking experiences in succession. Thank you so much for your help.

We'll be back in touch with you as soon as we have gathered together further information. It was so good of you to come in at such short notice, and in view of this situation. Many thanks again. Our unit will take you on now to the hospital if you wish. No trouble, the police dealing with the accident need to check up on how your husband is too. Only for their reports on the accident, and we don't want to put you to any more inconvenience."

The police car took me on to the hospital. I knew that all had to be well otherwise there would have been a phone call. He was going to pull through.

I had known when the surgeon left me in the corridor that Douglas would survive. It was because I had willed him to die and perverse as he was, he was going to live. After the recovery, he would return to his drinking, his thrashings and I had lost my chance.

Things did not quite work out like that.

TWO

Celia Philpott put down the phone resignedly. James had rung to say he was delayed. Yet another meal ruined. Celia and James's twelve-year-old son, Fergus, was away at Scout Camp. Her special Saturday tête à tête meal was now turning into another pathetic TV dinner on a tray. She blew out the candles and put the unopened wine back in the rack. She served two portions of the meal, covered one plate with film and placed it ready in the microwave. She had heard it all before. She sat down glumly to eat. Experience had taught her that there was no point waiting. He might not be home for hours. Being delayed, as he so optimistically called it, could mean a lot longer than a missed bus. He was on call, after all.

The phone rang again just as she sat down. She was going to have to take back what she had just thought. She looked toward the wine rack as she picked up the receiver, cupped the phone to her chin and stood up with the tray. She smiled at the thought of James ringing back to say he was sorted. In record time too.

"Is that Mrs Philpott, Celia Philpott? This is Miriam Coles, Andrew's mother. No, it's not Fergus, there's nothing at all wrong with him; I have just been talking to Jane Waterman at the Bridge Club dinner."

Celia breathed easier. Fergus and Andrew were at Camp together for the week.

"I am sorry to ring and bother you but, given the seriousness of the situation, I really felt I had to ring, you being the chairperson of the governors at St Peter's. You see, I heard this evening that Mr McIntyre, has been involved in a very serious car accident."

Celia clutched the tray she was holding. It teetered forward with her and the full plate began to slide. She managed to place it on the counter. She listened to the woman, but her replies were just mechanical answers to a lot of inevitable questions. A bizarre back and forth routine, that had no rhyme or reason, no depth or sense to it. Celia was in shock, but she somehow concealed it in her replies. Miriam Coles had absolutely no idea that the news she had imparted to Celia had shaken Celia totally rigid. Miriam asked her to inform other parents on the governing body chattering on and on. She went on to say that Jane Waterman had arrived in tears at the Bridge Club annual dinner. Miriam had realized that it was Jane's son-in-law, Douglas McIntyre, who had had the accident.

Once the phone call had come to an end, a terrible cold wave of fear spread over Celia. As she replaced the receiver, she knew that Miriam Coles had just loved being the bearer of dire news. Mrs Coles was a shallow busybody who spent her mornings shopping, her afternoons playing bridge and her evenings on the phone gossiping. Miriam bought her meals from a cordon bleu specialist who delivered to your door and even told you how to improve your place settings. She had a couple of cleaners, a gardener, an au-pair, a husband who performed admirably well at all the charity functions she organised; she had the model child, Andrew, whom she rarely saw, apart from to parade him at events or disgorge him from her Mercedes at school on her way to the shops.

Celia Philpott and Douglas McIntyre had been having an affair for just over two years. The simple reason why Celia had almost passed out when Miriam Coles had phoned her. There was nothing deep or even meaningful about this relationship with Douglas. She never, not even for one second, thought about Douglas, until his texts arrived. They were concise, 2.30, Waitrose, or 11.45, Little Chef. And if she could, her text would be even shorter, just acknowledging his, or giving an alternative time, in which case Douglas organized a meeting at the council offices, or a hastily arranged visit to a prospective parent at the time she suggested. He had a mine of excuses, and his secretary never rang him unawares. He told her and everyone else that he was allergic to phone calls, preferring texts instead. Celia could vouch for that too. So Mrs Gregg, the secretary, either sent a text or stuck a 'post it' on his computer screen. He was never away for longer than a couple of hours. At a maximum it got to two and a half hours. The staff, the parents, his secretary and the governors all marvelled at his efficient running of the school. His ability to fit in so much without giving any impression of being harassed just kept everyone in awe of him. He never lost his cool, he was a model of perfection as a Headteacher. His work as a part-time education lecturer earned him high praise. Celia Philpott always went home totally satisfied with his performance too.

It wasn't an affair, more of a gratifying of mutual requirements. They had known each other for a few years. He was the Headteacher of the school where she was chairperson of the governors. It was Fergus's old school. Celia had taken on the role to lighten James's load when the school had approached him. This chairmanship was a challenge she needed as Fergus grew up. Her professional relationship with the Headteacher was cordial and polite but they had never met at a social event outside of the school. That changed after they had been seated together at a Golf Club dinner over two years previously.

Douglas had been placed next to her at a large round table. They had shaken hands and smiled politely at each other before sitting down. She had first felt his leg brush against hers and thought it was an accident. Then, purely by chance, she had dropped her serviette and he graciously bent down to retrieve it for her, running his palm up her leg as far as he could go before brandishing the napkin and squeezing her hand as he returned it to her. She had felt a thrill of secret pleasure but looked at him innocently. She had no idea what would develop. He had been so charming, chatting to her and James across the table about all sorts of subjects. The rest of the people around the table were laughing and enjoying his company. His wife was seated opposite him, next to James. Such a pretty woman, Celia had thought. Douglas spent the rest of that evening stroking Celia under the table. So childish and totally ridiculous but she loved the thrill it gave her. She spread her legs at one point and had to lean forward to stop herself from sighing. At the end of the evening he had winked at her as he turned back to wave goodbye. She had felt like a teenager again. She knew that he already had her phone number. Within a week she got a text. No strings! DM. That was all it said. Celia spent a week hesitating about whether to reply but then she thought, "What the hell?"

She and Douglas met in supermarket car parks, in motorway services. They then got into one of their respective cars and drove to a hotel, and had quick, frantic sex. From getting into one car to getting out of it back at the car park Celia could set her watch that it would not be above that two hour span. It was on the same lines as one might energetically eat a sandwich to assuage a hunger pang, to fill oneself up without really thinking of relishing it. Just a means to an end.

Both of them had agreed to this deal, so a sandwich it was, once or twice a month, never more, sometimes twice in one week, then a regulatory month would go by. Douglas made sure that no-one asked any questions because there was no pattern at all to his sorties with Celia. That irregularity made it all the more enjoyable. They never talked of love or feelings. Both looked on their affair with the same indifference, which reminded Celia of the languid detachment she had remembered seeing on Mrs Robinson's face in *The Graduate*. It was doing no harm.

They were, after all, consenting adults. To Douglas it was quite as natural and ordinary as a round of golf, or a sauna; a relaxing interlude in between staff meetings and dealing with irate parents. To Celia, it was as refreshing as going for a swim or having half an hour on her walking machine. But she did especially like the risk element, and even more than that, she liked being the object of his desire.

James was so tied up with his work that he very often came home and quite literally fell into bed. He was asleep almost before his head hit the pillow. She loved James, loved her life as his wife and adored Fergus. But she just had to have that perilous addition from Douglas. It was her stimulus to give James his regulation dose of it and James loved the way she did that.

She was always especially good at that on the evening after she had been with Douglas. She regularly coaxed James on the same night. That way too, Celia was able to put Douglas out of her mind and body ... until the next time; all this was healthy. Celia felt that she was learning to arouse James through it. She made herself a reason to continue. She was actually kindling the flickering sex in her marriage into what a flattered James proudly put down to his remarkable sex appeal.

Suddenly she felt sick. She had never for one instant thought that Douglas meant anything to her other than the enormous satisfaction of being attractive to him. But knowing he was injured, maybe going to die? That threw a whole different light on the issue. It made her think about her feelings like she had never done before. She had never felt any guilt at seeing Douglas. Lydia McIntyre was fifteen years younger than her, and a stunningly attractive woman. Douglas was a year her junior and they had an arrangement. She wasn't hurting Lydia. She was probably helping things move along nicely for them. In turn, James got the best out of Celia because of Douglas; Celia really felt that Lydia must be benefiting from Douglas to the same degree. Sometimes when he came along to one of their meetings Douglas would be tense and on edge. Half an hour later he was in seventh heaven because of her.

She was brought back to the present. She knew in an instant that it was James who had operated on Douglas and she knew that that was why he was late. He was probably operating at this very moment! And she knew too that James would prefer to tell her face to face that Fergus's old Headteacher was lying between life and death. James's planet circled round Celia, Fergus and the hospital, but not necessarily in that order. James was kind, considerate, predictable and solid. All that was why Celia knew he would come in and sit her down with a glass of white wine and soda, and then gently break it to her that poor Mr McIntyre, whom he had met only last month at the Golf Club Annual General Meeting had been in a horrific car crash. Celia made a few mechanical phone calls, as Miriam Coles had asked her to do. She passed on the information as quickly as she could, finding herself able to repeat it dispassionately. Mr McIntyre was the Headteacher, she was the chairperson of the governing body. Douglas was a world away from being that same man. Mrs Philpott, the chairperson, wasn't the same woman who met him for sandwich sex. Celia definitely thought of herself as someone else when she was with Douglas. A warm, familiar arm curled around her waist and Celia felt the fear and shame within her pricking; James felt more like a phantom perched behind her very shoulder, knowing her inmost thoughts and they were too shameful to her now.

"Thanks for waiting up darling. Sorry about the meal. I'm afraid I've ruined things for you once again. I am sorry too that I feel I have to break our pact about my never talking shop."

James started to tell her gently about Mr McIntyre as Celia had predicted he would. Celia stopped him mid-sentence and related the phone call from Miriam Coles. James ate in silence as she spoke. She was able to do so much more easily than she had anticipated. Douglas and her liaison with him belonged to that secure padlocked part of Celia's sub-conscious. Like her memories of her first day at school – those vague snapshot sepia memories, which were far from being imaginary. But they were now blurred, faint, blotchy instants in her past. Douglas was part of that same sepia past now. Celia was beginning to wonder how she could ever get through life without him.

*

The following morning, I arrived at the hospital in the police car, ready for Mother's recriminations and scowls. Instead I was met with a sweet smile.

"I rang Anthony darling, he's on his way. He'll be here tomorrow lunchtime, isn't that kind? Now, don't look so surprised, you know how he dotes on me. The minute I asked him he said he would come, now how did you sleep? I took a Mogadon, I know I shouldn't have, but the idea of lying awake there worrying about Douglas just made me think, well, I have to be strong for Lydia too. So here I am. Goodness me, you look terrible, why don't you go and get yourself a coffee? Tell you what, bring me one back, no sugar. And don't you think you should get in touch with Heather in New Zealand?"

My mother never changed. Her conversation was always peppered with questions, which she then proceeded to answer. Mother was always more ill than you were, more in need of the doctor. Her being full of a cold was always influenza and no-one suffered more than her. And her adored Anthony had consistently put up with her spoilt ways. Somewhere in Europe there would be a business meeting to attend whilst he was over to see us. Jane would feed on this visit and refer to it for the next twelve months. Saint Anthony's visit, thank God for a son in her own image. Since leaving the UK, he could do no wrong. Come to think of it, it had always been like that, yet I didn't dislike Anthony for it. There was nothing to dislike about him. He was like father, detached from things, not musing over

Mother's words as I did. He just accepted her as she was and made the right noises when he was in her company, then got on with his own life in the intervening months between visits. He was the sensible one.

I adopted my safe, familiar muteness, while Mother doggedly filled in my gaps. Mother fervently believes that her replies are mine, just through my nodding or shaking my head or through the occasional yes or no which I manage to squeeze into her monologues. It is an easy solution for me.

Had I been a colour, I would have been a pale green or an ecru, never a wild red or a brilliant azure. Had I been an animal I would have been a deer, constantly afraid of the slightest movement, blending in to the background in my forest. Had I been the wave swirling over a beach, I would have been sucked greedily into the beckoning sand and vanished without a trace.

Both Douglas and my mother dominate me. I just let them do so. Despite this fairly damning self-observation I do not consider myself to be without character, feelings, or opinions. Both my mother and my husband have never taken that point into account, both being too wrapped up in the importance of their own discourse to care whether I have a reply to make. Being always one for the easier option, adopting the line of non-aggression, I have generally done exactly what everyone else wanted, because that line just suits my character and this world of self-centred people I belong to. Belonged to. Until yesterday.

There was the incident on the balcony which Mother was still unaware of.

Unbelievably, almost twenty-four hours had passed since then. I would have to tell her. The police might be coming to the hospital today. If they did, they would be asking me questions.

"Mother, I have something to tell you."

"Yes, darling, go on, I already know though, you don't have to think I haven't guessed. This is a lot more serious than you thought. The doctors have told you. I know dear, but you are young, you can recover, not like me when your father walked out. I just had to carry on alone. No-one would have looked at me on my own with two teenage children and a heap of debts. Yes, you have youth and childlessness on your side. Although, you will never find a husband like Douglas. Just be grateful ..."

"No, mother, not Douglas, no they haven't told me anything much yet. They can't, we have to wait at least 48 hours. It's about me, you see yesterday ...."

"Oh my goodness, how on earth can you mean to tell me that you think that anything concerning you could possibly be more important than this? Well what on earth can be the matter with you then? Why are you crying, stop it, STOP IT! That won't solve anything whatsoever. You, of all people need to be strong for Douglas and for me. You know, I am not getting any younger and this kind of shock can take its toll on an older woman. Stop it at once!"

Loud moans came rasping out of my body. The more she pleaded with me to stop, the louder I sobbed. Finally the nurse came along the corridor and asked me if I needed a cup of tea. A solution only the British use to defuse potentially perilous situations under the guise of it "doing one good". The nurse was used to frantic relatives; it was her job. So along came the tea and I sat there, still heaving, stirring it.

No other person in the world would have said that, only my mother. As the saying goes - where there's no sense, there's no feeling - and to none could it apply more than to her. She no more understood how my mind worked than she knew what I had eaten for lunch a fortnight last Thursday. And she cared not one jot about either. Had you accused her of being uncaring, she would have dissolved into tears and then just as quickly composed herself to be able to reel out a list of things she was convinced absolved her of such an admonishment.

Lack of caring? What about her bringing me up single-handedly, buying me the best clothes, paying for my big wedding. I should have a large letter 'S' on my back,

SELFISH, selfish to the last. The tirades were always along similar lines. She did more for me than I would ever know, did I not realise that if it weren't for her intervention, Douglas would have never even looked at me? She'd helped that along nicely. Otherwise I could have been a spinster, like her sister, my Aunt Agnes had been. And who had I to thank for paying for my education? The words rained over me. There was no use fighting, Mother had won another battle of words, her words, my silence. Her tone changed to a wheedling, sympathetic one when she realized I was not going to reply.

"Well, then, Lydia, what is it, you know that you have always been able to confide in me, just let it all out, dear."

"Mother, yesterday, just before Douglas had the accident, a girl fell from the balcony above ours."

"Oh my goodness, Lydia, you can't take on the worries of the world at a time like this, pull yourself together, think about what is going on here. And what has a complete stranger having an accident to do with you crying my dear, when your poor husband is lying in the next room between life and death?"

She spent the next ten minutes telling me I shouldn't be concerned about anything at the moment, only Douglas and his recovery. She was assuming as usual, Douglas would weather this particular storm and rise from his hospital bed like the Phoenix; he was, after all, the kind, thoughtful, doting son-in-law. She had total confidence in the surgeon; she knew of his wife through the Bridge Club. Mrs Philpott had a couple of friends who went there, and they said that Mr Philpott was married to his job. He put the patients before her and his son and his reputation was second to none, so he would do his level best for Douglas, and on and on and on. No more mention of the poor girl who had fallen. I wondered if it had actually registered with my mother at all.

As my mother babbled on, I recalled how the apartment above ours had been re-let a couple of months before and although I had heard high heels clicking back and forth,

I had never actually met the owner of them. Douglas had told me that they belonged to a young woman in her late twenties who worked in publishing in Cambridge. He had bumped into her in the underground garage; he said he thought we should ask her for drinks. That was so typical of him, as long as everyone around them both was there to reinforce the image of the bonded, devoted couple. She wouldn't be coming for drinks now, and Douglas wouldn't be serving them, either for her or for himself.

I pondered the situation. There were far too many balls up in the air at present to refocus on the matter in hand. I was brought back to reality and the hubbub of hospital life, with the arrival of James Philpott. I placed the cup and saucer down and looked at him as he came along the corridor. He was a tall, dark-haired man, looked around fifty. He had smile wrinkles around his eyes. I had already felt that he was kind, after our meeting the night before.

Damned Mother, who sailed into a plethora of questions, but Mr Philpott was deft, polite and clear. He would be able to answer any questions after he had explained a few things.

"Please excuse me, ladies, are you OK to come through to our Quiet Room?"

We went behind him, Mother clinging to his arm, telling him who she was, Bridge Club and the rest. She began beseeching him to make Douglas whole once more, spluttering at him along the corridor. He said not one word to crocodile-skinned Mother but smiled sweetly at her as he opened the door for us. We settled into the Quiet Room, furnished with outdated fabrics, swags, piping, ruffles and flowers. Wooden frames were nailed all over the walls, like little coffins. Thanks for this and that, dedications to loved ones who had sojourned on the ward. I found myself stupidly staring at one opposite: "In memory of Robert Cope, a loving husband and father, with grateful thanks to all the staff on Ward 7 for their kind support." I could not help the cynical thoughts. Mr Cope would be remembered little more than the swags and piping around the room by people like me. It was better to think those unkind things than to answer my mother back.

"As I said last night, the first 48 hours are crucial with this kind of head trauma. Your husband has sustained significant head injuries; if he pulls through, he will need a long recovery period. My advice here is to take it hour by hour."

This man was used to anticipating questions.

"A long recovery period means months, but he has the benefit of a huge support team here at the hospital and you will have help, don't worry. It is a question of small steps, and each day should see an improvement."

The surgeon went on to describe the other injuries. He spoke of broken ribs, extensive cuts and bruising and a perforated spleen. We were offered tea again by another friendly nurse who came in after ten or so minutes.

Afterwards I realised that she thus released Mr Philpott from his place there; he excused himself, asked us to be patient as his parting comment, said he would be on hand to talk to us whenever we liked. He then left the room before Mother had a chance to ask any questions. She would ask them later, she announced. How could this be, how could poor Douglas have this terrible thing upon him; what were we to do, who could we turn to, where would we end up now, with Douglas in such a state? And then the familiar abuse toward me, veiled with sobs and rebukes.

When she got no response, she launched into her own version of yesterday's events. Had I had an argument with him, what had caused him to drive off like that? Could it have been prevented, who was to blame, and before I knew where I was, she had managed to blame me for Douglas being not only in ICU but also for having gone out in his car, having even thought of driving. As usual, the words washed over me. Surf over sand. Sinking in, deep inside, wounding words which came pouring out of her mouth. They left no trace on me. I was able to remain as if unperturbed. I felt that she continued because she could see that I was not affected. I had had enough practice.

She did continue, like the yapping terrier does; and if perchance I had led Douglas to this because I was seeing another man, then it was on my conscience for ever. Had I no shame? She never even stopped for breath. The thoughts came into her head and straight out of her mouth, streaming forth. This was unbridled cruelty. When she stopped to regain her composure, she gazed into my eyes with sheer disdain. I looked behind her, almost through her, at the coffin-like plaques.

My phone started to ring. Mother's contempt for me switched to shock as she pointed to the sign asking visitors to switch off their mobile phones within the hospital. It was the D.I. who politely asked after Douglas and then asked me if I could call down at the station again when it was convenient. It was Sunday lunchtime. I said I would call later that day.

Mother's reaction was coupled with a sneer, when I calmly explained.

"So other people count before Douglas, how can you say it isn't a problem? What can you possibly do at a police station? Why don't they come up here ... ?"

"Be quiet, Mother."

I had actually told her to be quiet. So totally unlike the pre-yesterday Lydia. And she was, sitting there, open-mouthed. A newly-caught catfish has that same shocked expression. I stood up, and walked out of the Quiet Room, leaving her there. The dumbfounded fish on a boat deck.

I followed the black line along the corridor out of the building, out into the weak sunlight where I rang a taxi and stood waiting, glad to be away from both of them. I decided to make for the police station.

The inspector calmly asked me to go over the events of the previous day once more. I wasn't able to remember any more details.

"Mrs McIntyre, you said you heard scuffles, did you hear any other noise at all?"

I was drawn back to the balcony, to the scene of the washing flying past me, and it suddenly struck me, that it had been quiet, rapid but oh, so quiet. I knew what he was going to tell me, that this was suicide not an accident. "Forensics are carrying out further tests. That is why I asked you to come back down here. There are a lot of unanswered questions and you are, it seems, the only witness."

I had listened to him but not really heard what he was saying. I looked into his eyes as he said "forensics", and the full horror of it all hit me like a mallet. It was no use. I just couldn't concentrate. He went on but I just couldn't take any more. Finally I asked him if I could come back later, when I was feeling less shaky about the whole thing.

"I need to get some fresh air and try and come to terms with this whole thing. And maybe something else will come back to me, if I really think the whole thing over carefully."

I left the police station in a bewildered state and walked the mile or so to the flat, where I picked up my car; I had decided to drive over to Ely. I was free to go where I chose. No text message to send to make sure Douglas could monitor my movements. It was more than a pleasant sensation which swept over me. I gripped the steering wheel and thought hard about how the last 24 hours had provoked this maelstrom of emotions inside me.

As I stared up at the octagonal tower in the Cathedral, I caught sight of a crowd of young students walking around the building. Some of them were sketching, some were listening intently to the Verger who was explaining the history of the place.

"It is called the Ship of the Fens. Wherever you are around here you can see it rising proudly out of the flat lands of Norfolk".

It led me to think back to my own student days, sketching buildings in Cambridge. I was drawing that day when a handsome lecturer came to sit beside me. He leaned over and admired my work and asked to look at the other sketches in the pad. Then he offered to take me over to Ely and I saw that majestic vessel of Norfolk in a totally different light. As he drove back to Cambridge, he pulled his little sports car into a country pub and asked me would I like a drink in the tea garden there. We sat and chatted until early evening and when he dropped me off at my flat on that same evening, he strode round and opened the car door for me. He took his large hands and framed my face with them, giving me the most tender of kisses.

I married Douglas five months later.

THREE

Anthony Waterman looked at his watch and sighed. His mother had rung him yesterday for only the second time in seven years. The first was to tell him of Aunt Agnes's death and her plans for her sister's funeral. They included Anthony as principal guest. He had made the trip back and managed to fit in a short skiing trip to Courchevel. He felt detached from his family in England. He hadn't seen his father for fourteen years, although they did keep in touch now and again, but the contact was very much along the lines of that old friend you just have to keep in contact with "for old time's sake". It was certainly not father and son banter, as Anthony imagined it would be with others. He held deep down a strange feeling that if they were to meet, they would both regret the intervening years and wish they had made more of an effort to see one another.

As an adult now, he could see clearly why his father had left them. He knew that with his mother's temperament there could have been no half measures, no "arrangements". She would have screamed the place down if either he or Lydia had asked to see their father. Perish the thought!

Anthony was eleven at the time, Lydia fifteen. Jane spent a couple of years at the very least telling the same tale of woes to whoever came into the family sphere. Anthony grew through adolescence with that. Lydia didn't really figure in his life much after his father left. She was immersed in her studies and he had few memories of her when they had lived as a threesome. Then she had left home to go to university. Douglas had quickly appeared on the scene, taking Lydia out of their family picture. Anthony didn't care that much for Douglas. He had always felt that Lydia was under his thumb. She did as he wished, rather like his father had done with his mother, until that frightful day when he had walked out of the door and just never come back. Lydia appeared to enjoy being the dutiful wife. She seemed pretty spineless to Anthony.

The day he settled down, if he ever did, he would want a wife who was a partner not someone like his sister. Douglas decreed and Lydia agreed. Definitely would not do for me, thought Anthony.

And then there was his mother who was an insufferable pest. She must have worn his father down with her moaning and reproaches. It was all clear to Anthony now. In a strange way, the split between his parents had been the major reason for him succeeding in education and later on in job applications. Not long after he started his sixth form studies he had made a resolution. He would not remain in the clutches of his mother. He had worked especially hard at school and then at university, knowing that if he were to be able to escape too, he would need to have an excellent track record. He never looked back, only forward and he never regretted anything. His life was a busy, full one and nothing would induce him to return to the UK.

He now felt that his determinedness must mirror his father's. Yet Jane Waterman had no idea that Anthony felt this way. His success was hers; she savoured every accolade, as if it were hers and intimately believed that each diploma were her very own. She actually said it was due to her. She fed on his achievements and regurgitated them to all and sundry at her various soirées and functions. He knew that his mother sang his praises to his sister. "You should be proud of Anthony. He has real talent." Jane would pass around cakes bought specially for Anthony's rare visits and Lydia would nod her head and agree.

Still, that all belonged to Anthony's past and his past was just that, referred to, but with no nostalgia, just a matter of fact. He could stomach the odd cake and the gushing compliments if it kept his mother happy and at bay. Anthony mused over that as he nodded off to sleep. He was awakened with an enormous jolt. The plane had touched down at Heathrow and he had slept solidly for seven hours. That was a saving grace for him; being able to sleep anywhere, any time and making jet lag a thing he had rarely experienced. He collected his things together, exited the plane, across the tarmac, through customs, and into a taxi.

This was his first time back in the UK for three years. His mother visited him wherever his job took him. She had been out to Singapore a couple of times and he had arranged trips for her with his secretary. Anthony and his mother had taken a trip to Penang together and stayed in a beach-front hotel. His mother had loved it and spent the rest of her stay telling Anthony how wonderful he was. She rarely mentioned Lydia but Douglas was important for her. In a peculiar way, Anthony knew that he should be grateful to the man, for Douglas had replaced him in his mother's eyes.

Anthony got the taxi to drive directly to the hospital. He got out of the lift and took to the stairs, until he arrived at the ICU. As he strode down the corridor, he saw his mother coming out of a room. He watched her walking down the corridor in front of him. She had given birth to him, he owed her his mere existence, but what was there beyond that? He didn't feel anything at all, and it didn't perturb him, he wasn't ashamed. Suddenly she turned around and beheld him adoringly. He took her into his arms and she sobbed against him, wailed and moaned about how happy she was to see him, how poor Douglas was lying between life and death, and then she recomposed herself as she almost spat the words out.

"Lydia left me here yesterday. She is a wicked girl, she just went and left me. And she isn't here yet today and her poor husband is...is...oh, thank the Lord you are here, coming all this way, for her too. She is just like your father, never there when you need her. He abandoned me and so has she! What on earth are we to do?"

Anthony smoothed her hair and patted her and said the appropriate things. He asked her about herself, then about Douglas but what his mother said was not making sense. Finally, he persuaded her to let him take her for a coffee and they headed off for the hospital restaurant. As they pushed the trays along the rails in the restaurant, Anthony realised that he still didn't have the faintest clue how Douglas was or whether he would pull through or where Lydia was for that matter. He made himself choose an antiseptic-looking scone and butter, whilst Jane heaved and hiccuped with all the sobbing she had done, yet still managed to choose a cake and complain to the girl behind the counter about coffee being spilled into the saucer. Mother never changed, Mother needed everyone to circle around her particular planet called Jane, and with that she wasn't ever completely happy, but she was more tolerable. Anthony paused as he pulled out the chair for her to sit down and wondered how many times his father had held his tongue over the years.

Anthony, as a grown man, was just beginning to understand his father. He began to feel some respect for him too. Before he had pulled out his own chair, Anthony had resolved to try and revive the bond. He just felt there and then, that now was the moment, no regrets. He felt inwardly too that his father would welcome him. There would be no recriminations on either side. Anthony smiled at the idea of getting to know him. His mind came back to where he was and he glanced around the room as he stirred his coffee. A sudden grip on his elbow forced him to turn to his right. He looked up.

"Well I never, it's Tony, isn't it? I never forget a face, bet you don't know who I am, I weigh three times what I did the last time we met!"

Anthony looked up and saw a tubby face, but despite it, he still recognized David Diller who was, by now, leaning on the table, grinning at him. Anthony's mother, who was sitting opposite him, launched into conversation before Anthony had even drawn breath. She had recomposed herself, and told David in less than five blistering minutes how terrible life was for her and why. He agreed, commiserated, laid a hand on her shoulder and patted her sympathetically. Jane brushed the sleeve David had patted as if it were covered in insects. She kept silent for once, too horrified to do otherwise. The bloated friendly face then turned his gaze to Anthony.

"How long has it been? I know, it was at your sister's wedding, have bumped into her a couple of times over the years and asked after you, but you were always on the move, quite the jet-hopping executive, I believe? I've stayed around the place, you know me, never one for moving too far, I work in Cambridge now, got two kids and a mortgage for my sins, and this!"

He pointed to his belly and laughed out loud.

"Remember at the wedding, sneaking out round the back of the hotel for our first fag?"

Jane looked on disapprovingly, but, for once, said nothing. Anthony remembered that cigarette, more particularly its effect on him compared to David. The coughing, the spluttering, the feeling that this was the most disgusting thing he had ever tasted and the thought that it was the first and the last cigarette he would ever have. And it had been.

David was the planner and the schemer, the one who enticed him to try. David was in his class at school and when Lydia had said he could invite someone to the wedding Anthony had immediately thought of David Diller. Anthony had admired the reckless David more than anyone else in his class at the time. They had parted ways the month after Lydia married, when David's parents moved and he was sent to another secondary school in the town. They never met up again, simply because their paths never crossed. Anthony was steeped in his studies and David was absorbed in other pursuits, girls being the main one. He was married by the time he was 19. That was the last news Anthony had had of him, via Lydia. And here he was.

"Just been for a scan, got the most disgusting cough, just can't shake it off. Done the whole shelf of cough bottles at the chemists! Thought I'd pop in here and have a coffee, before I go back to work, got the morning off, might as well make the most of it! I'm a mechanic at the Audi garage, bet you're driving one, aren't you? Hey, I'm your personal repair man!"

At which point David, let out a throaty, phlegm-filled laugh, that said everything. Anthony knew that there weren't only the years separating them. Two teenage boys at a wedding, two totally distinct routes through life, two lives with no parallels, only uncharted differences. David sat down heavily beside Jane who was uncharacteristically silent now. She managed to move her chair sideways as he settled into his. She began to take an interest in the cruet set in front of her. David chatted on heartily about school days before he had moved house and they had found themselves separated. Anthony heard about people, whom for him were just familiar, but distant, names but whom for David were still people he saw as often as he had done all those years ago.

Anthony's blurred images of girls with pigtails and gym shorts, were David's clear ones of fat-bellied, tattooed women in ill-fitting hipsters, pushing prams around town. The conversation started to wane. David ran out of people he knew and Anthony ran out of the appropriate noises he had been making about them. He asked how long he was over for. Before he was able to reply, Jane intervened, thanking David for all his news and saying how they had to go.

"You see, Lydia's husband had had an accident," she said, standing up as she said it.

Gathering her coat and closing her bag, she terminated the conversation with the snap of that clasp. David started to push back his chair and stood up. As he began to back away, he wished them both well, then lumbered off with the predictable comment over his shoulder,

"Well, Tony, hope it isn't another fifteen years."

Another throaty laugh, followed by a spasm of coughing and apologies. Then he was gone.

"What an insufferable man, how can anyone let themselves get to that size, and did you see his fingernails?"

Jane went straight for the proverbial jugular with that unnerving nastiness. As they went up in the lift, poor innocent David was written off in a single blow. He was confined to that scrap heap of human lives. The title of a magazine which Jane could have edited with no problem whatsoever. No-one had called him Tony since those school days. Tony. Mother used to tell Anthony not to answer to it. When he was around twelve or thirteen he had asked her why she had called him that if she didn't like the shortened version. He only asked her once. She had launched into one of her fits of temper when all you wanted to do was to press re-wind and leave out the question you had just asked. Mother must have preferred to think of him as Anthony Quayle or Hopkins, than Tony Curtis or Blackburn.

Anthony was so like his father, Laurence. He would put up with virtually anything if it meant the quiet life he led would remain just that, undisturbed. He looked back to his childhood. Laurence Waterman was bending over his clay in the workshop and giving Anthony a ball of it to play with. Laurence was pushing him on the swing in the garden, Laurence was holding his hand when he walked to school, Laurence there, next to him, listening to him read. At that instant, Anthony could feel the pain his father must have felt. The choices would have been limited so he had cut his losses, preferred to sacrifice his bond with his children, than to juggle life apart with them.

Maybe that was why Anthony had never let himself get too involved in a relationship. As soon as he felt that things were getting serious with a girl, he pulled the plug on things. He had moved around the world too. That made promotion easier, and he had no problem finding girlfriends, but marriage didn't appeal. It meant commitment and he just couldn't do it. Someone had once said to him that men always chose women who resembled their mothers, that men often fell out of their mothers' arms and into their wives' clutches. What of the analogies to fathers? Anthony knew of none. At the first opportunity he would write to his father and ask for his phone number. And then before he went back to Singapore, he would go and see him. Anthony suddenly felt better. He could cope with Mother, after all, she doted on him and she always made a point of being less overbearing when he was around. He saw her so infrequently, and it was easier to give her sweet memories to feed on when he had left than to make her angry.

Too bad for Lydia, he thought, she has to deal with her much more than I do. I wonder how she feels about her? As the thought came into his mind, Anthony realised that he had never, ever referred to Mother in front of Lydia. There was some kind of barrier between him and his sister, that he didn't care to try and break down. She had her life and his own was so very different. Just because they had grown up in the same house didn't mean that they were bosom pals. He reflected on all this and realised that he hardly knew Lydia.

They left the restaurant and got in the lift, made their way back to the ICU. On arrival they were met by a nurse. Would they come this way, please? No, no, it wasn't bad news, just to let them know that they had just missed Mr Philpott. Jane squeezed Anthony's arm and said in a low voice,

"Oh, Anthony, do you think we might sneak off home for a couple of hours, I do so want to show you the new conservatory. I finally had that dreadful eyesore of a workshop of your father's flattened ... and we can't do anything here. They won't even let us in to see him. I need to find out where on earth Lydia is, what she is up to, when she should be here with Douglas; it really is quite unreasonable of her, selfish to the last that girl is. And I've got some of your favourite cakes in, do you know Hargreaves are still making them! I only buy them when you are over."

Anthony gave her an appreciative smile and thanked her, inwardly heaving a sigh. He had once said, only once, that he liked those cakes, and he got them every time he was over.

James Philpott walked into the lounge and slumped into the chair. Celia was out. Odd, no note. He had rung and told her that he was on his way home, as he always did. She had not answered or texted him back. Fergus had left a message on the answer phone, babbling excitedly about the Scout Camp and how he had fallen down an irrigation manhole, but he was OK; the Biology teacher had strapped his ankle up and forced him to take arnica as a homophobic remedy. James chuckled and made a mental note to explain one or two things to his son when he got back from Camp.

"Sorry, darling, I just popped out to the supermarket. How was your day?" said a flustered Celia as she pushed open the door. She had been to the supermarket, true, but before that she had taken a risk and driven by the hospital, wondering if she could find out about some more details about Douglas. But once she was there she was so afraid of being seen that she had changed her mind and driven right back out of the car park. Her phone rang and she saw it was James but she just couldn't answer it. She felt as if he knew the whole story.

As she drove home she wondered if she dared bring up the subject over dinner with him, but he would find that odd. They had their unwritten pact to leave work on the doorstep, like a pair of outdoor shoes. But, she thought, he had broken that pact last night. She considered her options feverishly. He had done that because it was someone they knew vaguely. Vaguely for him maybe.

Celia was more than flustered, she was perturbed too. There were so many unanswered questions. James and Fergus were her reality but Douglas and their stolen moments were the very reason that this reality functioned so well. One depended on the other; they were tightly associated yet totally independent one from the other. It was all over now between Douglas and her now. She knew that. It felt to her though as if their liaison had been discovered. Only that shame could equal the terrible guilt she was now feeling. Her ordered world had suffered a seismic change and no-one but her knew about it ... and Douglas. A totally brilliant idea came to her in a flash of inspiration. It was a way to bring up the subject without causing James to wonder why. She didn't even stop to consider.

"I have been thinking James, what do you feel about this, do you think it might be a good idea to get in touch with Mrs McIntyre and ask how things are? You know, as chairperson of the Governors, I really believe it's up to me to inform the parents and staff officially about Mr McIntyre? And I'd much rather find out that way than ring Miriam Coles and get the news second-hand."

"That is so kind and thoughtful of you, Celia. Yes, a very good idea. Ring the ICU and tell them I gave the go-ahead to release her phone number. If she's not happy about it when you ring her, you can blame me. She looks totally lost. I saw her this afternoon, and her mother is there with her. Not one bit of help at all. Quite the reverse actually, poor girl was having to deal with the woman crying and moaning when I saw her."

It had been so easy. Celia breathed slowly out with relief. She knew nothing of Douglas and his private life at all. They never talked about their lives away from the hotel rooms they met up in. There was nothing sordid about that either. Celia felt a huge pang of remorse now that it had all come to a halt. She fixed a drink for James and he motioned her towards the bedroom. That was unthinkable; she was trying to stop thinking of Douglas not revive the memories.

"Darling, do you mind awfully, if we don't, I just feel so off colour, I wondering if I am not coming down with that bug that is going round the playgroup?"

Celia worked as a voluntary helper at the local playgroup, so she was able to come and go as she pleased there, she was an extra pair of hands but totally expendable. That gave her the kind of freedom she needed. She didn't need that freedom in quite the same way today. Every part of her life was all so totally awry that she felt giddy. It was easy to say she was "off colour", not too far from the truth at all. She wasn't that at all; she was totally wrecked.

She was however able to successfully put James off for today and manoeuvre her way out of things. And he himself had unwittingly given her the green light to ring the hospital. She would do that and find out about the ... the Headteacher. She winced as she thought of making the call, but it was a means to an end. She would phone, get her mobile number and then call his wife. His wife. Celia had never stopped to think once about her before.

She made a lame excuse to James about just popping out to pin a notice on the school gates and went out. She drove for a few miles and pulled into a pub car park. People were leaving after their Sunday lunches; Celia sat in the car as she had done so many times before. She wasn't waiting for Douglas this time. She fished the phone out and rang the ICU.

*

"Mrs McIntyre, we have reason to believe that Claire Leaver was murdered."

I had returned from Ely and gone back to the police station. I looked at Boswell and swallowed. This was awful. Thinking that the girl had had an awful accident was terrible. The idea of a suicide was more dreadful but I had somehow or other digested that in my own mind. Now he was telling me that someone could have killed the poor girl. I didn't know what she looked like, didn't even know whether she lived alone. I knew absolutely nothing about her, and she had been murdered right above me. While I was sitting on the balcony thinking of a plan, someone put that girl's life on this earth to an abrupt and horrible end. She had been tossed over that balcony like a used paper cup.

There was something so very shocking about it. I was on my balcony when that girl was pushed over the one directly above mine. I looked down at my feet and started to cry. I thought of my mother's non-reaction when I had told her; it had been a little like the response you have when you watch a TV murder, when you are thinking as the suspense increases, oh it's only a play, only actors, not for real, gosh but the scene was so realistic. This scene was for real, and now here I was being told by Boswell that the girl had been murdered.

"She was dead before she fell, Mrs McIntyre. She had been strangled. What I need you to do is to try and think very hard if you can remember anything at all, not just before but maybe during the morning, or the previous night. You see, for the moment, the only other witness we have is the young man who was jogging. He has testified that he saw your husband leaving the garage entrance around 2.05pm, just before he found the girl."

I looked up at Boswell. That didn't correspond with the time he had left the apartment at all.

"The jogger was the person who phoned 999. He was running past the flats towards the beach and nearly tripped over the ...."

Boswell stopped short.

"The other flats which face the promenade are either empty, or the owners were out at the time. We have interviewed a lady who who was walking her dog along the promenade, but she didn't see anything at all. She came forward this morning, after she had read the account in the newspaper and she remembered hearing the sirens. Just let me re-cap here, you say you had never met the young lady?"

"No, we intended to invite her round for drinks, my husband said he had met her once in the underground car park, he asked me to organize it, I just hadn't got around to doing anything. I was thinking of it."

Pathetic, I thought, as I wiped my face. I was imagining the girl's last moments, and I didn't even know her name.

"And I am sorry to say this, because I know you are in a state of shock, what with the accident, but ..."

He looked closely at me. "We will need to speak to your husband as soon as he is out of the artificial coma. You understand, he could have a vital clue. He could well have met her killer in the lift, or in the car park as he left. The forensics man has just now confirmed to us that Miss Leaver was strangled shortly before, before ...," he hesitated, "... before she was found at 2.10pm."

A convenient euphemism for the girl's ultimate resting place: that paving slab outside the flats. That passive voice "was found" almost took away the horror of it all, certainly it made it more acceptable to the ear. She *was found* after she *was seen* hurtling past the balcony. And now she *was placed* on another cold, cold slab. Would Douglas be joining her there? The thought was there, at the forefront of my mind.

I wondered what the girl had looked like, whether she had been pretty. What had caused someone to want to kill her and then push her body over a balcony. Did that person think people would assume she had jumped to her death?

"Your husband might be able to tell us something. He left the flat at 1.30pm, you said?"

"Yes, I am pretty certain of the time, because we always eat at 1.15pm at the weekends and I had been running a little late."

I knew the exact time, almost to the second. Douglas was furious because I was ten minutes late with the lunch, and then I spilled the soup...he had walked over, put down his empty whisky tumbler and calmly taken the tureen out of my hands and placed it on the worktop bar. Any spectator would have thought that he was going to take me in his arms and smother me with kisses. The blows rained down on my head, then he slapped me about the face and stormed out; the beating had lasted for around five minutes.

"Had you been on the balcony since he left?"

"No, I went to the bathroom, and, and... I washed my face...because I had been crying."

I struggled and hesitated over my words, recalling the moments after Douglas had left. I had walked over to the bathroom, sat down heavily in the wicker chair, and held my head and wept. Then I had stood up and looked at myself in the mirror, dishevelled, wild, my face streaked with tears. I had turned my head to the side where he had struck me and had seen a tiny rivulet of dried blood tracing downwards. I was shocked at that, and pulled over the magnifying mirror to examine it more closely. It was coming from my ear or more precisely from my ear lobe where the earring had been squashed into the base of my scalp. It had drawn blood at its puncture mark. I had washed the spot and wiped away the blood. My next thought had been to hide it, which was relatively easy with my long hair. I had pulled my hair forward and combed it cautiously, then looked again at myself and down into the sink as the pink water curled away. I had placed both hands on the sink and drawn fingers inwardly into two fists until the knuckles whitened. This was to be the very last time he would lay a hand upon me.

I had walked out of that bathroom in a different frame of mind. By the time I had opened the balcony door, and sat down on the chair, the decision had been made. There was no other way forward. How long I had to wait to perfect the plan was irrelevant. At least now there was a goal. This was what it was all about, just to know a way forward gave me so much solace, healed those wounds, made sense of my life. How much time had been wasted! How many times had I been sure that he would change? How often had I blamed myself for being the one who had aroused his anger? How many times had I thought that I must behave differently? That I had to become the wife he wanted! Yes, I had to change, but not for him, for myself.

46

"I can imagine this is hard for you, but did Mr McIntyre say where he was going?"

"No, no, he left in a hurry. He never said where he was going. Where did the accident happen?"

I couldn't bring to mind whether the little policewoman had told me where the accident had happened. I had committed none of that meeting in the hallway of the flat to memory. All I could recall was the phrase, "how lucky he was, because the angle at which he had hit the wall had saved him". Maybe I had willed it to happen, because at the very moment he had had the crash, I was planning to put an end to my miserable way of life in the only way I thought possible.

"It was on the straight stretch of the A324 to Ely, about a mile before you reach the town."

I knew exactly where it had happened. I had just been to Ely and back. I had actually passed the spot *twice*! I felt a cold frisson roll over my entire body. I explained what I could remember, then left his office once again.

From Boswell's office, I walked out into the sunshine and over to the car. As I was getting in, the phone rang. This has got to be Mother, and I just can't deal with that at the moment, but out of that curiosity most of us have when our phone rings, I took it out of her bag and looked at the screen. "Caller's name withheld". I pressed the accept button.

"Mrs McIntyre, this is Celia, Celia Philpott. I'm the chairperson of the governors at your husband's school. I just got your number from the staff nurse on the ICU. You see, my husband said that he thought that it would be OK for her to give it to me. First of all, please let me say how sorry I was to hear of the accident. I am sorry to disturb you like this at such a difficult time, but I thought I should ring and ask how your husband was. You see, the parents are ringing me and I ...I ... I want to give them correct information. I don't want anyone to start off rumours. And the staff and parents are wanting to send some flowers to the hospital, but...and they wanted to know how you were, and whether you needed any practical help..."

Her voice trailed off.

"Thank you so much for ringing, yes, kind of you to ring. Yes, I'm OK. My husband is not out of danger. He is still in the ICU; he hasn't come round yet though. They have put him into a drug-induced coma to improve his chances of recovery. The surgeon"... I hesitated ... "Mr Philpott, your husband ... says he could make a full recovery but that it will be a long road. He really can't say at present. The first 48 hours are crucial."

*

Celia rang off, arranging to ring Lydia in a couple of days and saying she would post a notice at the school gates and inform the school secretary. Celia thought she had a kind voice, a young, innocent voice. Douglas had never once mentioned her. Their respective lives were only intertwined by this one thread. Celia already knew that she would never be with Douglas again. Now that she had made contact with his wife, she felt enormously guilty, as though the news about their affair had just been posted all over the town. As she sat in her car, she was aware of people around her, and almost reddened at the idea of what she had done over these two years. She thought of Fergus and James and what she had risked. She had had a lucky escape. What a ghoulish thought, while he was fighting for his life and it was her husband who had been his saviour! There was no going back now, that was part of her past, her sweet hidden past.

FOUR

Laurence Waterman was in his workshop in Gran Tarajal. It's a town in the south-east of the island of Fuerteventura, far removed from the tourist track being between two developed areas. It is directly opposite the African continent. Morocco is less than 60 miles away. When the Chergui wind blows, sand from the Sahara settles everywhere. The island owes its name to this inhospitable wind, for Fuerteventura means strong winds. There are a few dusty bars and two hotels behind the seafront in Gran Tarajal. Narrow streets wind upwards to the church and a leafy square. The fishing port is at one end of the town and the marina next to it houses small, unpretentious boats. Nothing to speak of as a place, but Laurence has made his home there. His fame and fortune as a sculptor came along around two years after settling there.

Laurence now lives in a small town house at the back of which there is a garden with aloe vera bushes spiking upwards here and there. Across the street he also owns a sprawling set of outbuildings which house his workshop and some of his earlier and present works. He trained in ceramic art in the UK, and as a young artist he had become quite successful. He had met Jane at an exhibition in Cambridge. His first creations were on show there: asymmetric patterns on wavy vases. He had just won a prize from his art school for the most promising newcomer. He was producing these vessels with a new firing technique he had developed. After this initial success he had had a couple of large commissions and he and Jane had married the following Spring. Lydia and Anthony were born around the time when his creations had moved into another phase. He was still using the same firing technique but the vases had turned into quirky teapots with babies' legs and arms about them. The lids had angelic, chubby faces beaming up at you. They sold well all over the world. Laurence was thinking of his own two children when he created them.

There were examples of them in many ceramic museums across the globe. He made and sold them for over ten years, but tired of the technique and the repetition and yearned for another inspiration. While he was awaiting that moment which all true artists need, the family had fallen on leaner times. He had been forced to recall quite a few pieces from the same museums in order to keep body and soul together and, more importantly, Jane at bay. After a good few months' hardship, Jane had exploded. The huge argument had left him shaking and despondent. A week or so after this dispute she had marched into his workshop and told him to pack his bags. She told him that she had had enough and shown him the door. He had left quietly that same evening with only a small attaché case of sketches. As she had closed the door behind him, he had walked off and left his children sleeping in their beds, without so much as a kiss because Jane had refused to let him go upstairs. He had no idea where to go or what to do but he had not disputed her throwing him out. He had dealt with the awful blow just like he had accepted the downturn in the popularity of his works. He looked on both events with the same inherent calmness and acceptance. He had welcomed his achievement at the creation of his works and rejoiced at the wonder of his children. But he could not bear the pressure which Jane placed on his shoulders. All that mattered to him was being fulfilled in what he was doing. He had tired of those teapots with their chubby legs and plump cheeks and had stopped making them completely. There had followed a bleak period where he wondered what he could possibly do that would satisfy him like the thrill he had had when he produced that first piece. During that period Jane never ceased for one minute to badger him.

Finally, when she screeched her derision at him in his workshop and told him to go, that is just what he did. For Laurence, there followed a terrible period of remorse and loss. His wish to create dwindled away and he had no direction. However, the romantic tale of the true artist finding inspiration really happened to Laurence. One day he was cutting through a pomegranate; as he placed the two halves on the table, he looked closely at them. He did not eat the pomegranate halves but instead stood up and drove straight into Puerto del Rosario. He walked into the largest builders' yard where he negotiated a price on an industrial cement mixer, a delivery of one hundred 50 kg sacks of cement, six lorry loads of gravel, and twenty rolls of wire mesh. He made an arrangement with the salesman to pay the bill at the end of the year. That gave him six months.

Within five days, he had made his first pomegranate. A monumental basin weighing 5 tons, hand-hacked with an axe he had for chopping the dead palm leaves off his trees. He used a dark-brown pigment and added resin to the cement mixture. His first creation was born. Later he made a variation and wound rope around the drying cement fruit, which he removed after a day, producing deep whirls. He was on his way to another creative victory and he knew it. Not that it mattered to him. Paying the bill was possible even if he couldn't sell these, because he still had nine of those cherubic vessels in museums across the globe. He would just recall them and that was that. What was important to Laurence was that thrill of creating.

Those giant basins were a huge success. People clamoured for them. Huge sculptures for their gardens, each one an original by Laurence Waterman. One day a letter from the French Embassy in Tunis arrived, asking him to bring his basins to a ceramics exhibition which was to be held in their gardens. So he sent five basins off to Tunis and took the plane from Fuerteventura to Madrid and then on to the North African capital. The whole city captivated him. The sculptures were the uncharted hit of the exhibition. Not only that, but the Embassy bought two to keep. The other three had been sold before Laurence's plane had landed back in Madrid.

Naseera and Hakim came into his life quite by accident. He was 59 by the time he went to the exhibition in Tunis and he had not looked at or approached another woman since Jane had thrown him out almost fifteen years before. After three weeks, Laurence had chosen to go to Fuerteventura, where an artist friend of his had offered him the use of a house he had there.

"Use it as a bolt hole, Larry, you need a break."

Laurence thought long and hard while he was there; he came to the conclusion that every visit he would make to his children would be a visit controlled by Jane, on her terms. Laurence knew that whatever he did, he could not win any competition in those stakes. He gave in to it and did exactly what Jane did not expect. Jane wanted a fight, a struggle for control, for custody even, but Laurence was not the fighting type. After he had spent a month there, he came back to England to arrange shipping some things out to the island in the Canaries. It suited him as a place. The scenery reflected the way he felt: empty, barren, deserted. He had found a place to rent in Gran Tarajal and if things worked out he would buy something there. After less than a year he bought a house in the same village which had lots of space and lots of, what the agent called "potential". Laurence felt that he could be himself there. He felt saddened by the loss of his children, but he knew that he had no other choice. The geographical distance from them helped him to accept the separation more easily. So he had left England for good and behind him his wife and children. According to Jane, who was beside herself with rage when she realised what he had done, he had welched on the marriage, abandoned her and her offspring. It certainly gave her every opportunity to berate him wherever she went. Jane dated his abandoning them from the moment she had opened the door and almost put her foot behind him as he walked over the threshold.

Laurence knew he had taken the least pugnacious option and in doing so he had given up his children. Jane had won, as usual. So he lived alone and sent Jane regular cheques to cover hers and children's expenses. He didn't keep a record, didn't declare it to the tax authorities, didn't seek to benefit in any way from giving her over half of his income. Because of Jane, he couldn't have a relationship with his children, but they would grow up and one day he might be able to hold them in his arms and let them feel his tears on their cheeks. And he was a patient man.

Whilst he was in Tunisia for the exhibition, he went visiting and took the train down from Tunis to El Djem, where the real Coliseum lies. He was walking around the exterior when a small child ran up to him and held out his hand. A girl came from behind and took the child's hand, admonished him for begging and excused herself to Laurence. She pulled the little boy towards her and walked off. Strange, thought Laurence, most of the children here are encouraged to beg. He spent the afternoon marvelling at the place almost untouched by tourism as he knew it in Fuerteventura. As he got back to the train station, he spotted the girl and her little charge. They got on the train and sat opposite Laurence who immediately held out his hand to the little boy. The beady black eyes widened and the boy chuckled loudly, looking up at the girl as if he needed her to accept the joke too.

"I brought my little brother here to see the wonders of Tunisia," she said, in perfect English.

By the time they had got off the train, Laurence had learned that Naseera and her brother Hakim lived in Tunis with their aunt and uncle. Their parents were both dead and Naseera had become Hakim's self-appointed mother. She was 18 and he was 7. Their parents and three other brothers had all been killed in a house collapse after a gas explosion two years before. Naseera had been out at the market with Hakim buying vegetables when it had happened. Laurence spent the next three days with them, meeting their aunt and uncle, dining with them and visiting those unknown parts of Tunis that the dwellers still keep to themselves. By the third day, an idea had formed in his mind: he could ask Naseera and Hakim to come back to Fuerteventura with him. Certainly not as a wife for the idea was preposterous to him. He was almost three times her age. But he really felt that could give the two of them something. His offer of a home meant that could see to it that both of them were educated as their parents would have wished. The idea took hold of him and he smiled at the prospect of opening his home to them. This was a truly altruistic gesture and it was what he wanted more than anything.

He did not dare to put the idea to Naseera. He went back to Fuerteventura and wrote a long letter to her aunt and uncle. In a second letter to her, he stressed that there were no emotional ties to his proposal. He felt he could give something back, that his own children were grown-up, one married and the other working abroad. He went on to add that he had no other links and he wanted, he needed company, young people around him. He ended up the letter saying that the few days he had spent in Tunis had made him realise how lonely he was back in Gran Tarajal.

Naseera's aunt wrote back and asked him to come and stay with them for a month or so. Naseera didn't reply, but her aunt said that she was thinking over the offer. Laurence went to Tunis at her aunt's request. A month later the three of them flew back to Laurence's little haven. Their agreement was that Laurence would help them both in their education in return for ... nothing at all.

Now, six years have passed, Hakim is 13 and Naseera 24. This unlikely trio live in Gran Tarajal, and Naseera works as a secretary at the Marina. Hakim is in high school and doing well. No-one bats an eyelid as to whether they are companions, or father and daughter and son or what they are. Naseera has three languages at her fingertips: English, French and Spanish and she helps Laurence with the business side of his work. She does the books for him, contacts clients, writes articles for the Press when exhibitions are coming up.

She has dragged Laurence into the 21st century from an electronic point of view. His dusty fax machine has been replaced with a state of the art computer. Laurence still spends time sitting in his workshop contemplating his new designs. He has not tired of working with cement, and alongside his pomegranates and whirl-coated basins there are other immense sculptures, hand-hacked with the same axe. Hakim helps out at the weekends and loves Laurence as any son or grandson might. He can barely remember life in Tunis; his parents and brothers stare out at him smiling from the only photograph he and his sister have of the family they lost.

Laurence insists that the two go back to Tunisia at least once a year, but as each year passes, he can see that they are becoming more and more Spanish in their outlook and attitudes. They race across the airport to Laurence when they arrive back and fling their arms around him. Laurence feels pride at this strange little family which he chose to create and who chose to accept him. And they walk towards the car park, hand in hand, happy to be home again, Hakim chattering and Naseera asking questions about Laurence and how he is. She cares, Hakim cares, this is what life is all about, thinks Laurence.

Anthony Waterman and his mother went back to her house; while she was busying herself in the kitchen, Anthony cautiously phoned his father. A young boy's voice answered.

"I am sorry, Laurence is away at an exhibition in Oslo. Who's calling please?"

"It's Anthony Waterman. No, it doesn't matter, when will he be back, please?

"I'm not sure, just a second, I'll ask".

There was a pause and then the boy said,

"He'll be back on Wednesday evening. I'll tell him you called. He might ring tonight, just thought, would you like his mobile number?"

Anthony declined and thanked him then said goodbye to the boy. He didn't want to ring his father in Oslo and disturb him; all he wanted to do was ask him, tell him that he wanted to see him and that he wanted to book a flight to the Canaries to spend a few days with him. But his father was going to be away until Wednesday. Anthony sat down in the lounge at his mother's house and wondered how she would take it if he told her. He was not prepared to go down that particular emotional roller coaster.

He could look into a flight to Oslo. That might be a good idea - on neutral ground. He had no idea what the hell his father was doing living with a young woman and her son and he didn't care. It was not any of his business. When Laurence had written to him, about six years before, he had just said that they had an *arrangement* that suited them both and that he was very happy. He had said that the little boy was the girl's brother but Jane had told Anthony that he was her son from a childhood pregnancy and that Laurence was covering up.

She had made such a fuss about it all, that Anthony had preferred to just let it all slide. In any case, his father had not invited Anthony to come and stay with him, but there again Anthony would not have had the slightest intention of going anyway. Six years ago Anthony had been 25 and had just taken up his first job. He was working in Cairo for the Egyptian government on a health scheme for young mothers. The fact that his father was living with someone meant absolutely nothing to him. He couldn't even properly remember what his father looked like. Anthony had wondered for one brief moment what the *arrangement* might include but when his mother came out to see him in Cairo, she made no bones at all about setting that record straight.

She had always known that Laurence had had an eye for younger women; Laurence would stop at nothing for his own gratification, Laurence had always put himself before anyone else, and she had been left to pick up the pieces and deal with bringing up his two legitimate children alone. So saying, she implied that there were hosts of *illegitimate* ones roaming the planet. Anthony made one comment over that hour-long character assassination of his father. He praised her warmly for what she had done as a single mother and Jane preened her proverbial feathers, once more thanking God inwardly for Anthony, who might bear his father's name, but who was so much like her. That comforted her for she felt that Anthony had not been so profoundly influenced by Laurence. After all, she would say to him, he was only 11 when his father had left them, whereas Lydia, at 15, well, she was just like her father in every respect, and always had been.

Anthony's own gentle character was not really reflected in the work he did. He was under intense pressure in the professional side of his life, involved in selling infant food products to countries whose female population had little say in what their children consumed. They either lived in famine-hit areas, or the trend for ready-prepared foods was not the norm yet in under-developed countries. He was passionate about his work, because he really felt the company's campaigns in those countries were making a difference to people who needed and deserved help. He got the odd e-mail from Laurence as did Lydia but neither he nor Lydia had ever sought to further their relationship with their father. The spectre of Jane's wrath kept them from doing that.

It was an odd situation because Anthony resembled his father so much, both in the physical sense and in terms of character traits. He was tall and lean like Laurence. He had the same wavy fair hair, the same piercing blue eyes, the same angular face with high sculpted cheek bones. He had a quiet disposition, he was gentle, not given to outbursts of anger. He was, like Laurence, almost self-deprecating at times, always avoiding confrontation, preferring to back down rather than to go in headlong. So you would have thought that Jane would have disliked him because of that inevitable similarity to the hated and reviled Laurence. But she didn't.

On the other hand, Lydia, who looked nothing like her father, was constantly reminded of how alike him she was by her mother. Lydia was small, almost bird-like. She too was very fair-haired and she had pale green eyes. According to Jane, she looked like Laurence's mother, her grandmother, who had never figured much in their lives. Grandma Waterman lived in Leicester and was not able to drive. Anthony could recall visiting his paternal grandparents on odd occasions with his father, before Laurence had left them, but his mother never went with them. He didn't know why.

His grandfather had died very shortly after Lydia had got married but the three of them had not attended the funeral. He didn't know why either. As it came back to him, he wondered why his mother had not taken them to it, or why his father had not got back in touch to take them along either. He didn't even know whether his father had gone to the funeral. After that, there had been no more contact with his grandmother. She became a remote figure belonging to his early childhood; a tiny lady with a sweet smile and a high voice. After his grandfather's death, there was no more mention of her. Anthony had always presumed that his mother didn't get on with her, so that after his father left, there was no reason for her to keep up the contact.

What Anthony and Lydia did not know was that Jane had resolutely refused to speak to both Mr and Mrs

Waterman both during and after Lydia's wedding. She had thrown all the letters and birthday cards that the little bird-like grandmother had sent each year to Lydia and Anthony directly into the bin. Before doing so, she had pocketed the money contained in those same envelopes. Laurence had rung her to tell her of the arrangements for his father's funeral but she had told him firmly that they were all ill with 'flu. She did not inform either Lydia or Anthony about their grandfather's funeral until a week after it had taken place, telling them that they had not been invited.

A year after Mr Waterman senior died, Laurence had rung her once again to tell her he was placing half of the proceeds he had received from the sale of his mother's detached house into Jane's bank account. It was a considerable amount of money as prices were high and the property was a very desirable one. Jane believed that the money was her right not a gift. Laurence also asked her if she would mind if he sent on a trunk of memorabilia for the children; he and his mother had carefully sorted through things before she moved into the flat. To his great surprise and relief, Jane had agreed instantly and put the phone down very quickly, once he had settled with her when it was to be delivered. He was happy that for once she had not created a fuss. What he didn't know was that her hurried agreement was due to a prior engagement. A taxi was just drawing up outside the house, bound for the airport; Egypt and her cherished Anthony was her destination. And what he would never have dreamt either was that on her return, Jane had ceremoniously burned that trunk and everything it contained on the same bonfire she had lit to dispose of the clippings from her overgrown laurel hedge. She had smiled triumphantly as the photograph albums curled up and caught fire. When the lace baby clothes had blackened and withered in the heat, Jane felt like she had cremated Laurence himself.

Anthony began to think that the idea of flying up to Oslo was a great one. That way he wouldn't have to tell his mother anything and that was one enormous plus. Anthony could just invent a meeting, stay overnight in the capital and be back on Wednesday evening, with more than enough time to spend with his mother and sister and visit the hospital as well. His return flight to Singapore was booked for Saturday; he had taken a week off but he could do some work from wherever he was. There was a conference call booked for later that evening, when it would be early Monday morning in Singapore. He hadn't seen Lydia yet, but he had only been there since lunchtime. My God, he thought, I feel like I've been here for weeks.

*

Kind of Mrs Philpott to ring, I thought as I replaced the phone in my bag and started up the car. I would have to go up to the hospital and face Mother. That was the awful part of having asserted yourself with her. Rather like having to walk back into a room after you had marched out and slammed the door. You always have to open that door and go back in, so you lose every time. You have to backtrack, take the blame. Mother was like a terrier, she would continue about how ungrateful you were until eventually you just capitulated. Snapping at your nerves, just like the annoying dog nipping at your heels. I pulled into the hospital car park and walked up to the ICU and looked around. Mother didn't appear to be there. A huge wave of relief flooded through me as I went up to the nurses' station; a young nurse looked up from her notes.

"Hello, Mrs McIntyre, did you manage to get a bit of a rest? No news, I'm afraid, well no change, I mean. By the way, we have a bag of your husband's belongings here. They should have given them to you yesterday. I know, it does look terrible, everything in a bin bag like this, but we have to make sure that we don't lose anything and, when the patient comes in, we just have to be as quick as we can. Some of the clothes will have been removed in the ambulance, and then they all go into a bag. So everything your husband had on him at the time of the accident will be in there too. And do be prepared because some of the garments could be bloodstained and certainly they will have cuts in them. The paramedics will have cut them off your husband you see."

I took the bag from her and mumbled my thanks. The only thing to do with the clothes was to throw them away, but I thought that I had better do that when I got back home. It didn't feel the right thing to do at all to open it there and then. I decided to go back to the car with it. I felt strange walking back out of the ward carrying all of Douglas's possessions and clothes in a black bin bag. It was almost like disposing of him. I held my breath at the thought.

*

Anthony had borrowed his mother's car to drive to the hospital. He booked a flight to Oslo as he sat in the car park; he had decided to go to Norway but had also decided not to let his father know. That way, he was not covering up to either of his parents, and that made him feel better. He was just not saying who he was going to see. If he got there and couldn't find Laurence, he would visit the city. He was convinced though that he would be able to see his father. There could only be one exhibition of garden sculptures, only one place where they could house them too: the Vigeland Sculpture Park. Anthony had managed to book a flight from Stansted, so he could be there in around an hour. He was pleased that he had made the decision. He left the car and the first person he saw was his sister, closing the boot of her car.

*

"Lydia, Lydia!", called Anthony across the car park.
I turned around and saw my brother running towards

me. I was taken back to a day long ago on the beach when Anthony and I were playing together and he ran across the sands, shouting to me. He was skipping across the surf. Those were my memories of Anthony. He was there in front of me now, panting a little. I hadn't seen him for three years. We hugged nervously. It was strange to be walking along with my brother. I told him of the morning's altercation with Mother and how I had left the hospital abruptly rather than have an argument. Anthony told me he had left mother at home preparing a meal. She was expecting him back for dinner.

"What do you feel about coming back for dinner too? There's no use you staying here, and it would be better than being on your own."

I would have much preferred to spend a third evening alone, but I felt it was only fair to Anthony to spend the evening with him. I agreed and called Mother to let her know that we would both be coming back. Jane asked how Douglas was.

"Lids, I am going to Oslo tomorrow evening, I'll be back on Wednesday evening," said Anthony, "then I am due to fly back on Saturday, but if ... if you need me to stay, I can always change my ticket."

I looked round at him and thought how kind a face he had. I was so touched that he had made the trip. He had dropped everything when he got the phone call from mother and caught the first plane out of Singapore to the UK. He had thought about me. I felt now that I could count on him. I walked up the stairs next to him and wanted to squeeze his arm and thank him but for some inexplicable reason, I didn't dare. Instead, I told him of the events on Saturday afternoon, of the fact that I had been spending time down at the police station, as a witness. He listened carefully to me, and I knew he was feeling immense pain.

As we arrived at the floor, Anthony put an arm around me, and said,

"I had no idea, does Mother know? She never mentioned anything, I just thought you had gone home for a break from ... from the hospital."

I knew he was thinking of me having a break from her when he said that. That had been a familiar tactic with both of us. No point going on about how Mother was; it didn't change one single thing.

We went into the ICU, and put on the gloves and gowns and hats, then opened the door into Douglas's room. He was swathed in tubes and monitors. His head was wrapped in a netted bandage and both eye sockets were swollen and puffy. The nurse who was monitoring him smiled at us; we stayed for a few minutes, talking in low voices. There was something of the feeling of respect you have when you go into a church. Douglas would not wake with those muffled voices, yet still we spoke in hushed tones, as we all do when visiting the sick.

Outside, in the corridor, we sat together and when there was a lull in the conversation. I asked him what there was on in Oslo. He told me that he had arranged to see someone there. He did not elaborate. He was leaving in the morning and he would be back late the following evening. We drove back in the two cars to mother's house and the evening passed off quite well. Anthony talked of his promotion and life in Singapore. Mother listened intently to him and gazed lovingly across the table at her only son. Towards the end of the meal, I excused myself as I was so tired and was about to leave when Mother said,

"Lydia, what about you taking Anthony to the airport tomorrow morning? I'll go up to the hospital and you can join me there. Anthony, if you take my car, I might need it, and leaving it on the airport car park will cost you as much as Lydia making four journeys. Anthony needs to be on top form for his meeting in Oslo, you know."

Anthony looked over at me and we both agreed that it was the most sensible solution because it was such an early flight. Before I had time to really think it over, Mother made up the spare bed. My idea of a peaceful night in the flat alone had turned into a dinner for three at mother's house and a practically sleepless night on the lumpiest bed

I had ever known. The following morning, we got into my car and I drove Anthony over to Stansted. Just as we were approaching the airport, he said,

"Lydia, I have something to tell you. I'm going to Oslo to see Father, I just decided yesterday. He's there for an exhibition and I just suddenly decided that I wanted to hook up with him again. I rang him and his ...the ...a boy answered the phone and said he was away in Oslo till Wednesday, so I just made a spur of the moment decision."

I smiled and said, "Oh, Anthony, I wish I were coming with you!"

And I really meant that, to actually see our father again would be wonderful. I had not given him one moment's thought for years, but there he was, in my sweetest of memories, at the wedding, the kind-faced, Panama-hatted man who had arrived at the house in his crumpled white linen suit about an hour before the ceremony. Mother had hit the roof.

"You are not going into the church in that, how could you, oh how could you? I just hope that this is some kind of sick joke!"

I had silently thought he looked rather cool, a bit of James Stewart or Cary Grant about him. Suave and tanned, his hair longer than it should have been, curling around his collar, and the only man at the whole wedding in a white suit, and the only man in a Panama hat! He had his way, as mother put it, he had come in the one suit and the one suit it was; afterwards Mother complained vociferously that he had managed to ruin her day, all the photographs and consequently the whole wedding.

I was inwardly delighted that he had annoyed mother so much. I had the delicious feeling that he was so very, very proud when he walked me down the aisle; he had leaned over to me as we went though the church archway and conspiratorially said,

"Darling, Lydia, take your time, the chances are that you will only do this once in a lifetime, savour it, enjoy it and SLOWLY does it, let them look at you, you are so beautiful!"

As we drove into the airport, I left the engine running at the drop-off zone, and got out to kiss Anthony goodbye. I went around to the boot where he was taking his overnight bag out. As he did so, I caught sight of the dustbin bag with Douglas's clothes in it that had lain there all night. I had forgotten about it completely. We stood together for a moment, unsure of each other, both unused to kissing goodbyes, brother and sister, but man and woman at that moment, unaccustomed to each other's ways in this kind of situation. Finally I broke the few moments' silence and said,

"I'll go home from here, and get changed now, and I'll be back to pick you up at 9 tomorrow evening. Safe trip! And say hello from me too!"

I drove home and thought about Anthony, on a plane, to see father after over fifteen years. I wondered whether he would be pleased to see Anthony. The memories of my father stopped on my wedding day. Every time I thought of him, I thought of that day, when I had gone from a nervous girl into a nervous bride and wife. The day my life had become Douglas's, when I stopped thinking for myself before I had even really begun to do so. So young, and now approaching middle age.

As I parked the car in my allotted space in the underground car park a chill spread over me; this was where the girl's killer had been. I looked around tensely, took the bag out of the boot and walked swiftly towards the communal bins at the back entrance of the building. As I lifted the lid, for some inexplicable reason, the nurse's words as she had passed me the bag over to me yesterday came back into my mind,

"*So everything he had on him at the time of the accident will be in there too.*"

I closed the lid and walked back over to the car with the bag. I stood for a moment, then decided to empty it there and then. Taking it up to the apartment was like taking him back in there. I quickly unlocked the boot and tipped everything into it. I surveyed the bloodstained trousers, a shirt which was in shreds, a pullover cut down the centre, socks, underclothes. This was an awful thing to have to do. This was Douglas there, not his clothes. I felt nauseous as I touched them, as if I were laying my hands on his body. It was a terrible task. I began to imagine what it must feel like to do this when the person is actually dead and felt a wave of angry disappointment flooding through me. That feeling made me so ashamed but the more I tried to push it out of my thinking, the more it took hold of me. I was truly hoping he would die.

I started to stuff the things back into the bag. Mechanically, my hands went into the trouser pockets just as if I was checking them before throwing them into the washing machine. I felt some keys. His school keys! Then, in the small, inside zipped back pocket a plastic credit card wallet which I didn't recognise. I finished putting everything back into the bin sack and lifted it out of the boot to go back over to the bins and dispose of it. I was relieved to have dealt with it and just wanted rid of the things now. On the floor of the boot, I caught sight of a small shiny red mobile phone. This wasn't Douglas's phone. His phone was a larger black iPhone. He had left in such a rage that he had not even picked it up from the hall table. It was still there now. Then it came to me. Anthony must have left this phone when he took his bag out of the boot. It must have slipped out of an open pocket in his overnight bag. Anthony would be airborne by now, or he might even have landed. He could be worrying about it. I thought it over; I had no idea where he was staying. I had his phone so there was nothing I could do to get in touch with him. I would have to wait until he got in touch with me or until tomorrow evening when he returned.

After putting the three items, the wallet, phone, and keys into my shoulder bag, I walked back over to the bins. I was still thinking of that little phone. It was one of those cheap ones that you can buy with a pay as you go card. Perhaps Anthony had bought it to use in the UK whilst he was over. It certainly didn't look like the type of phone a top executive would have had. Perhaps it had been with Douglas's things? Whose was it then? Could it belong to a child at his school?

It seemed a more plausible reason. The children weren't allowed to have mobile phones at Douglas's school but more and more of them were getting them for Christmas and birthdays now and some parents had already asked Douglas to revise the rules on having them. He had been thinking it over and had already mentioned to me that it was on the agenda for the next Governors' meeting.

I decided to ring his secretary to tell her that Douglas had confiscated a child's phone. I just felt like I had to tie up all the loose ends. Dorothy Gregg knew everything about the school and Douglas depended on her for most things. Like so many secretaries, she ran the place and Douglas, like so many managers, took the credit for being a superb administrator. I needed to phone her about the school keys anyway. I was so weary. I got up to the apartment and heaved a sigh. It was only 9 o'clock in the morning. I had been up since 4.30am and had slept for about an hour before that time in that dreadful bed that mother had had since we were children. I remembered that Mother would be up at the hospital by 10 am and would be expecting me to be there already.

I'll just lie on the bed and have half an hour ...

I slept for five hours and awoke in a panic, with that awful feeling one has when one oversleeps. For a full minute as I struggled to come back into wakefulness I didn't even know what day it was, never mind the time. Yes it was Tuesday, 2pm and mother would be seething. I had unplugged the landline the afternoon before, because I was afraid that the local newspaper might try to ring. It was, after all, a juicy story for a local rag, with the local headteacher critically injured and his wife witness to a murder on the same afternoon. I had learned from Douglas that I had to be very careful about what I said to whom.

My own bag with my mobile in it was in the kitchen. I got up and switched on the landline and went to get it. I should ring Mother, I really should. I should ring the hospital. I should let the school know how Douglas was. As I sat in the kitchen thinking of all these calls I had to make, I remembered the other phone and the school keys in my bag. I rang St Peter's school first.

"St Peter's Primary School, Mrs Gregg speaking, how can I help you?"

"Hello, Dorothy, this is Lydia McIntyre ..." I got no further.

"Oh, Lydia, thank you so much for ringing, how are things, we are all so worried. You see, we've had some information from Mrs Philpott, but I so wanted to speak to you. I am so very very sorry. We didn't want to disturb you, but the parents are ringing, and rumours are flying around. The children are asking questions and we are all so worried. We have got a huge card going round the school and all the children are signing it, well it started like that but some wanted to draw things as well as write their names, so it has turned into quite an epic".

She chattered on and on about staff collecting for flowers and cleaners wanting to know what was the best thing to do, could they visit, should they send a card too? She said she had just been waiting for me to ring.

"What is the situation?"

I was ashamed to think that I had not been at the hospital for almost 24 hours, and I hadn't rung in either. I was truthful yet non-committal, saying she was on her way up there, and would give Mrs Gregg a fuller picture later on in the day. I explained what the surgeon had told me and how these first 48 hours were crucial.

"I have come across Douglas's school keys and a mobile phone in his things and I was wondering if you needed the keys at all and whether I should bring them in with the phone. I am assuming that Douglas must have confiscated the phone from a pupil, because it isn't his."

There was a pause at the other end of the line, and then Dorothy Gregg said,

"Well, that's very odd. No, the keys can't be his school keys because they were in the usual place at the caretaker's lodge yesterday morning when we opened school. I came in half an hour early because I had heard the news and I thought there would be quite a few extra phone calls. And I wasn't wrong there. You see, Mr McIntyre always leaves them here, in case ... in case he gets burgled I think. I suppose they could be a spare set, but he has never mentioned that to me".

In other words if she didn't know about them, then they couldn't be the school keys. Dorothy Gregg was thinking as she spoke, and I knew it.

"You say there is a phone? Well, to be perfectly honest, I can't think it could be a child's because he would have told me on Friday. I do all that kind of thing, get in touch with the parents, you know and field them away from direct contact with him unless it is absolutely necessary. He definitely doesn't keep a phone if he does confiscate one. He gives it to me and then I ring the parents and ask them to collect the phone on the same night. And I leave a post-it on his computer screen to say the phone has been collected. No, he doesn't keep them. You see, it is a very tricky area that, we are not supposed to confiscate them at all, because they could be stolen and then where would we be? As a matter of fact it is a thorny issue altogether and Douglas, sorry Mr McIntyre, I mean, he had decided to set the record straight at the next Governor's meeting and get a definite ruling on it."

I had stopped listening to Dorothy Gregg. At least I knew now that the phone was Anthony's. The call had cleared that up anyway. I thanked his secretary and promised her that I would ring in the near future with an update on Douglas. I clicked the off button and sat down at the breakfast bar. I felt around in the bag and touched the keys and pulled them out. There were three of them on the keyring. As I fingered them, I thought that I recognised two of them. They were the two keys to the apartment, the upper and lower locks! How silly of me to have thought they were his school keys. I just hadn't looked at them properly. Why on earth would Douglas have an extra set of keys to the apartment? And where were his other keys, the ones with the car key on them? Then I realised they were probably still in the car; they would still be in the ignition. A feeling crept over me that I didn't like, the feeling that perhaps the keys were at the breakers' yard by now. The car had to be a write-off. I shivered.

Before the invention of air bags, Douglas would most certainly have died. His car had six of them. I had no idea what had actually happened to cause the accident, other than the fact that Douglas had hit a wall and seemingly swerved in the right direction at the last second as if he had known he was going to hit it. Mr Philpott had said that the angle at which the car had hit the wall had saved his life. And no-one, not the detective, nor the surgeon, had mentioned the fact that Douglas had been drinking. I wondered again whether they had breath-tested him. They must know, they would have taken blood samples. And what was this third key, smaller than the other two. It looked like a freezer key, or a locker key. I didn't recognise it at all.

I put them down on the worktop and looked at them. They were together on a keyring which I had never seen before either. A leather fob, with an open hoop on it, a hoop that was dangling, because it had come loose. I touched the silver hoop and pushed it on my little finger. I looked carefully at the leather. I could see the holes where the hoop had been attached and had come loose. I straightened it on the worktop and looked at it again in the position it would have been in if it had been attached; it wasn't a hoop at all, it was an initial - a silver letter C. Could it belong to someone else, someone who Douglas knew, and he was holding on to it? Didn't sound plausible. I was puzzled.

As I looked at the initial, my mobile rang. It was Anthony.

FIVE

Celia Philpott drove carefully through the town centre. She was driving more slowly than normal, because she had things on her mind. She was trying to concentrate on the road but she was feeling more and more guilty. She just couldn't get the sordid nature of the whole affair out of her mind. Douglas's accident had polarized things. It was of course the end of things between them, but the beginning of a sort of inner torment that was consuming her as time passed. She could not focus on anything any more.

James was at home. He had taken the day off and had wanted to take her out for lunch, but she had refused. He had booked the restaurant, a quiet little country pub which had just got a Michelin star. Celia had read the article out to him about the place and said how much she would love to try it out. He was puzzled as he rang to cancel the reservation. Celia was not herself at all and he could not understand why. She had said she was coming down with a bug, but had spent half the night pacing up and down in the lounge. He had got up a couple of times but she had told him very curtly to leave her alone. She had never ever spoken sharply like that to him before and he was hurt and disturbed.

Then this morning she had gone out whilst he was in the shower and not even told him where she was going. They had both looked forward to this week when Fergus was at Scout Camp. Last week Celia had even said, with that tinkling laugh of hers, as she was packing Fergus's things, that James could start preparing for his second honeymoon starting from Friday night. And on Friday night, they had made passionate love. Celia had told him he needed to keep his strength up because Fergus was away for a whole week! They had laughed together in bed and he had felt so very close to her and so very much in love. Now, three days later, he was sitting alone in the kitchen, wondering where in Heaven's name she had gone again and what had gone wrong between them. He racked his brain, he had no idea what had happened to cause such a radical change in her behaviour.

He started to think over what could have caused this. Was it his involvement with his work at the hospital? They had often discussed it and Celia had told him over and over again the she was 100% behind him in his dedication to work. She had stressed that work, his kind of work, had to come first otherwise he would not be able to maintain the excellent reputation he had at the hospital and among his colleagues in other hospitals. She encouraged him to further his research work too; she searched the internet for him, looking for fellow colleagues who were researching the same field of brain surgery. He regularly had calls for other doctors, asking his opinion on cases, and he gave monthly lectures on unusual cases to medical students in Cambridge. Celia was always so proud of his achievements. He was very involved in his job and sometimes felt that he had neglected her. Over the fifteen years they had been married, things had wobbled along in the bedroom for much of the time. Once Fergus had been born and they had been told that it would be unwise for Celia to go through with another pregnancy because they had discovered she had lupus. Both James and she accepted the situation, discussed adoption and arrived at a mutual conclusion: they had Fergus and he was healthy, they were lucky and they would leave it at that. Theirs had been very much a joint decision, openly discussed. James went for a vasectomy and Celia said how much she appreciated him doing that. James privately hoped that it would revive Celia's interest in sex, once the fear of getting pregnant had been removed. It didn't, and then quite suddenly, about two years ago, she had asked him to take her to bed one afternoon. A change occurred, a radical change in Celia's attitude , a change for the better, the much, much better and it had happened literally overnight. One day she was the same mildly interested, let's get this over with Celia and the following day, she sent him into paroxysms of sheer joy. She started initiating things and James was thrilled. He wondered what he had been doing wrong up until then, but decided that he had got it right now, and he looked forward to going to bed, even when he was dog tired. Celia had worked out how to arouse him. Until Saturday, that was, when she had told him she felt unwell, and since then she had been distant with him, sharp on occasions and absent for a lot of the time. He was saddened by the change in her and worried about her too.

James was preparing to go back to the hospital when Celia arrived back. She walked in and just walked on past James as if he weren't there. He caught hold of her sleeve.

"Darling, please try and tell me what's the matter, I know you aren't yourself, is it something I've done, tell me please!" James was almost begging her.

Celia looked stonily at him, through him. It was such a look as he had never seen the likes of. A blank glare, which froze him physically, which made the hairs at the nape of his neck stand on end. It made him think that this woman in front of him actually hated him. He drew his outstretched arm away and it hung limply at his side. He was suddenly afraid. And he had not one clue as to why this was happening. His whole married life, his happiness, seemed to be crumbling around him. His wife had changed within the space of a few days. As Celia looked at him, he felt unable to ask her anything else directly. He was terrified of what she might say or do. He had lost confidence in her.

They stood facing each other in silence. Finally the eerie theatrical pause was interrupted by Celia's mobile. She jumped and pushed her hand into her bag, scrabbling around to find the phone. James loved her message on her answer phone, 'excuse me for not answering you, I *will* ring you back, I'm just looking for phone in my bag, as usual!' It stopped before she could answer it. She flung the bag resignedly onto the kitchen table and walked off towards the bedroom. She hadn't even checked the phone to see who had been trying to ring her. What if it were Fergus, thought James. He looked into her bag and saw the phone still illuminated, with the missed call sign. He pressed the button and the initials DM came up. That didn't strike a chord with him; he was just so glad it wasn't Fergus. He followed her, and as she opened the door, she turned around quite viciously and bellowed at him,

"Can you not just leave me alone, do you not understand what I am saying to you, just leave me alone!"

And she leaned toward him and actually physically, pushed him away from her, swivelled back to the door, opened it roughly and slammed it shut behind her. He was dismayed. This was another woman shouting at him, a woman who had changed within the space of less than three days. For James the only way forward seemed to be to avoid her. To leave her alone. He rang the hospital and told his secretary that he would be attending the afternoon clinic today as there had been a change of plan at home. He set off for the hospital profoundly troubled. This was supposed to be his day off with Celia; here he was going in to work to get away from her.

He had no idea what to do. They were a loving, happy couple, or at least they had been, and this thought made him uneasy. He had thought "had been" quite unconsciously, "had been", implied that it belonged to part of his past, that it was a former existence, that it had ended. He just didn't know what had happened. He racked his brains to try and make an explanation seem possible and drew a complete and utter blank. He got out of the car at the hospital and walked into the building with deep, deep foreboding. For the first time since he had met Celia, he was having doubts about their relationship. Thunderclouds had formed over their marriage. He was glad that Fergus was away. He then remembered that he had still not told Celia of Fergus's phone call. He was so glad that the missed call to Celia had not been from Fergus. He wondered how the boy was; he had told his father that his ankle was strapped up, so James started to wonder whether or not Fergus had been able to join in all the activities. He thought he should give the Scout leader a call, and made a point of asking his secretary to remind him to do it after the afternoon clinic session. As he walked into his office he realised that it had not occurred to him to phone Celia and ask her to do it: something that was unimaginable before last Saturday.

Laurence Waterman just loved Oslo. There was a cleanness about the city, a feeling of space and order. The people were so welcoming to him. He felt appreciated and respected. He had not intended for his work to become well-known because he created mainly for his own pleasure. However, he could not deny that he enjoyed it when people appreciated his endeavours. Naseera had helped him enormously in the administrative side of his business. She had turned it into a viable enterprise, in fact. He would never have come this far without her support and encouragement. It was doubly important to him now as an older man. At the back of his mind he could not help thinking that if Jane had helped him like that, he would never have...but each time those thoughts came into his head, he strove to stop them developing because they were negative. He felt deep down that he should never have any regrets. The wish to work for inspiration had drawn his family life to an abrupt and sorry end. The need for it had turned him into a single man overnight.

He had overseen the installation of his exhibits. They blended in perfectly with the austere landscape and the other monumental pieces on permanent exhibit there. Vigeland had made a wonderful park for Oslo. He had met a few other sculptors and he had been approached by a French magazine to do a photo shoot in his own workshop at home in the Canaries. He had also met a landscape gardener who was writing a book on the gardens he had created. Adriano Bertoletti was so impressed with Laurence's work that he told him he wanted them to collaborate on his next venture and that he intended to include that collaboration as the final chapter of his book.

Laurence was flattered and pleased with all the attention he received. He was able to give Adriano a card with his website and his e-mail. There was a further invitation to exhibit in Venice in September. That was to be a huge affair, turning St Mark's Square into a sculpture park. There were to be all the logistics of getting the exhibits there by barges. Laurence knew he could put all the organisation and coordination for that into Naseera's hands. How fortunate he was! Naseera had explained to him that those cards would be useful and had reminded him to take a dozen of them with him to Oslo. She was his right arm in the business side of his work, which did not interest him in the slightest.

He truly thought of her and Hakim and their house as home and family. They had been together as a family for six years now. When he had first arrived in the Canaries it was to stay in a ceramist friend's holiday home. Laurence was literally homeless. Each house had an identical hot tub in a postage stamp garden. Each had a satellite dish on a false terracotta roof. After staying just outside Corralejo for a couple of weeks, on an estate with 799 identical holiday homes, he was ready to get on the plane back to the UK. He had no home and no plans either. Corralejo was a place he hated for it was noisy and smelly and felt like Leicester with sun. There were huge TV screens in all the bars, not a Spaniard in sight and signs in lots of European languages but no Spanish. He could not wait to get out of the place.

After a few days, he hired a car and travelled around the island. He discovered that the rest of it was nothing like Corralejo. He visited the southern part and found the same hotel complexes as in the North, but it was less raucous and brash. He liked Morro Jable on the southern tip but it was too near all those hotels. Laurence was making his way back to Leicester with sun one hot afternoon when he happened on a town that was to change the whole course of his life. He took a right turn off the main road about an hour from Morro Jable and landed in Gran Tarajal. This was Spain, deep Spain and he loved the feel of the place. It was an immediate reaction, a bolt from the blue, a love affair. He rang his friend that night, thanked him and said he would be leaving the holiday home at the end of the following week. He rented a little house in GT, as he called it, and bought one in the same narrow street the following year. He made quick friends with many of the local people who were curious yet not intrusive. "El Inglés" was the man who lived alone and never had any visitors.

He had made a point of learning Spanish straight away, going to classes, taking private lessons, forcing himself to join in group activities so that he could learn the language. He had now arrived at a plateau in his language development, but he could converse about the weather, the food, the materials he needed for his work and that sufficed. When Naseera and Hakim had come into his life, the vehicle language had been English and so they spoke English at home. Hakim had learned very quickly. He continued, naturally, to speak to his sister in their native language, which Laurence encouraged because he told them their heritage was part of them and to be cherished. Hakim went to primary school there and picked up Spanish very fast, being immersed in it. Naseera had taken private lessons and then enrolled in a secretarial course at the local college. She worked harder than anyone in her group and managed to pass the exams even though her Spanish was not at all perfect. She was determined. Laurence had always felt that she would go far and she was proving him right. She had taken the job at the Marina on a temporary basis, helping out over their busy period, but they had offered her a permanent post; she was too good at her job!

He phoned home on his second night in Oslo and Hakim chattered on to him about his marks at school and how he had come first in the 400m race in the sports lesson. He asked Laurence about Oslo and Laurence told him all about the exhibition and the old part of the town. Hakim asked if he wanted to speak to Naseera.

"Hello Laurence, did you get a good night's sleep? Have you managed to eat well there?"

She was always so concerned for him, Laurence felt truly that this was his family.

"Laurence, your son called last night. Hakim spoke to him but he didn't leave a message. He just said he would get back in touch."

After the call Laurence sat down on his bed in the hotel room and thought about Anthony having rung. It had been so long. He was surprised. He wondered if there was something wrong. The last time he had seen Anthony had been at Lydia's wedding, although Naseera had set up an e-mail for him now and some kind of connection where he could actually see people as they were talking. Laurence had not used it yet, but he wrote very occasional e-mails. Their lives were so separate. Laurence had tried when they were both younger but had had no response from either of them. There wasn't that much he could say, their lives had no common links that they could converse about. Family was out, TV programmes too, books, well Laurence had no idea what Anthony's tastes were. Current events, well that was rather like scraping the barrel, thought Laurence.

After his father's death there had been a change in his feelings; the children had not attended the funeral, even though he had written and offered to come and get them. He offered to pay for a hire car for Lydia or Jane to drive over there. He had been deeply hurt. His mother had been distressed too. They both wondered what had happened. Neither of them believed that the children and Jane had 'flu. He and his mother had cried together when Heather had made the trip back from New Zealand and his children didn't turn up at all.

Laurence had wondered if Jane had anything to do with their non-appearance but he would just not let himself believe that she would be so wicked as to have stopped them from coming. He sent cheques every birthday and Christmas to both his children, always via Jane, so that she could actually see that he was making that small effort, but he didn't hear back about them. Anthony had moved around so much that Laurence lost track of the new addresses, so it was much easier to centralise gifts via Jane. He didn't mind, he knew that Jane had brought his children up and that he had been absent. He couldn't expect his children to come running now after all these years. And he didn't expect, or indeed want, any gratitude from them for his having financed their education — this was their right, not an option for him, and he had been glad to do it, knowing that he had given them the same opportunities that his own parents had given him when he had gone to Art School. Lydia being married had meant that she had forged a life for herself and her husband and Laurence was not part of their sphere. When his mother had decided to move into the little flat, she went to the solicitor's with Laurence and the considerable proceeds from the sale of the large detached family home were split in half. Laurence received a quarter share of the proceeds. He sat down in the solicitor's office and wrote a cheque to Jane for £65,000. It would help pay off some of her mortgage.

Jane had also succeeded in convincing Douglas how base that side of the family were. He had privately told her that he would not let Lydia be tainted by the riff raff on her father's side of the family. Little did Laurence know that Douglas took over from Jane in intercepting Lydia's mail. Lydia never knew her grandmother had wept over the grand-children's absence at their grandfather's funeral. Lydia had only found out he had died a week after he had been cremated and her mother made sure that Lydia realised that her grandmother had not wanted the three of them there, had insisted that they left her alone to grieve – that the three of them were not welcome. And when they learned from their mother that she had developed Alzheimer's, Jane told Lydia and Anthony that the symptoms had been coming on for years.

Anthony landed at Rygge airport and took a taxi straight to the Vigeland Sculpture Park. He asked a couple of people about the Waterman sculptures and was directed to them. He got a real buzz from knowing that his own father was so well known in this field. It was all so very strange; here he was in Oslo when a couple of days ago, he was sitting in his office in Singapore, wondering what he would make for his evening meal that night. His mother had called him in tears and spluttered on about the accident. He had left the office and gone directly to the airport, not even giving himself time to go back to his house and pack. He had bought an overnight bag at the airport and two complete changes of clothes. Up until then he had never had many lingering thoughts about either of his parents, his sister or her husband. One parent had been omni-present, suffocatingly so, whereas the other, reviled by the former, had been omni-absent. He didn't have any particular aversion to his sister but their contact was so infrequent that he felt that his secretary knew more about him than Lydia did.

So much for nature and nurture. A heap of old bull's bollocks, thought Anthony. I have not been in Father's company for longer than five bloody hours and that was almost sixteen years ago! And yet I feel something so deep inside for the man. What's it all about? He stood in the park looking at his father's sculptures. Monolithic columns and shapes rising out of the ground, calling to him. He was visibly moved by them and felt glad that he had made this trip to Norway. It was almost lunchtime and he thought he had better try and find the man who remained etched in his memory. Laurence was there in Anthony's mind, but now he needed to see him, to feel him, to be with him. He had just over 24 hours.

He was leaving the Park and heading for the centre of Oslo, thinking he would make for the Tourist Office and get them to phone some hotels to see if Laurence Waterman was staying there. He caught sight of a poster advertising the day's conferences, and there it was in black and white, Monday April 15th 2013, Laurence Waterman, conference in the Oslo Kongressenter, starting at 2pm. Laurence was giving a conference this afternoon! Anthony was beside himself with excitement, so he got a taxi into the centre of Oslo and walked happily into the Congress Centre. It was 1.55pm. He went into the large hall and took a seat near the front of the stage, near enough to see the people up there clearly. He was shaking with excitement. He knew then that he had done the right thing.

A talk in Norway at 2pm means exactly that. Anthony had been one of the last to take a seat in the packed hall. At precisely 2pm, a young man with a pony tail walked onto the stage ... to thunderous applause. Anthony looked at the programme he had picked up in the entrance. He re-read the events for the day, he couldn't find Laurence's name there at all. He was puzzled. After a few minutes he excused himself, shuffled past several annoyed conference listeners and walked out, back into the Congress Centre foyer, over to the main desk.

"I am here to listen to the Laurence Waterman conference, but ..." He got no further.

"So sorry, Sir, that was yesterday at 2pm."

Anthony was totally shattered. He had read the notice and thought it was Monday today. So much for travelling halfway around the globe and supposedly never having jet lag. How crassly stupid of him! He cracked his fist down on the counter and said "Damn!" in a very loud voice. The girl looked at him. A shocked expression spread over her face. She was certainly not used to people being so upset at missing a guest speaker. Even though Laurence Waterman was appreciated in his field, she thought that this man was going a bit too far.

Anthony apologised to her and asked her could she help him to locate Mr Waterman, that it was very important. The girl went behind into the office at the back. He could see her looking at him as she spoke to another man who came out to the front desk, smiling acidly at Anthony.

"Good afternoon, I'm the hotel manager. Our receptionist tells me you are looking for Mr Waterman. Would you please mind explaining why you need to see him? Is it urgent? Don't you have his phone number or his hotel?"

There was mild irritation in the man's voice, a slight air of disbelief about him. He looked Anthony up and down suspiciously.

"Look here, I can prove it; Laurence Waterman is my father," said Anthony, taking out his passport as he said it. He was beginning to feel angry as he thrust the passport forwards across the counter, pointing at his last name. The manager was effusive in his apologies, offering to ring around the hotels to see if he could locate Mr Waterman. After the fourth hotel, he replaced the receiver and said,

"I am so sorry, Mr Waterman, er ... your father ... checked out of the Grand Hotel at midday; apparently he is on his way back to Madrid this afternoon."

Anthony was crestfallen. He thanked the manager and turned away; as he walked out of the Kongresscenter he felt totally dejected. As he walked away, he wished he had not been so impetuous. He was stuck there now.

Laurence decided that flying back to Madrid a day early was a very good idea as he had seen the exhibition, met lots of interesting people for Naseera to contact for him, done the talk and he just wanted to be back home. He would stay the night in Madrid and get the first flight back home tomorrow morning. He had rung Naseera back after their phone call and told her he would be home a day early. He was missing them too much and the next time he went away, he told her, I would like you both to be with me. He got her to book him into a hotel at Barajas Airport. She organised his connecting flight for the Tuesday, changing it from Wednesday.

There was little else Anthony could do now as he had missed the flight back to London. Lydia was picking him up at Stansted tomorrow. The only thing to do was to book into a hotel for the night and do as he had thought he would do if he hadn't been able to see his father: visit Oslo. He had absolutely no wish to do that at all now. He booked into the hotel next to the Kongresscenter and went up to his room. He thought he would phone Lydia and tell her. He was so disappointed and she had been so excited at his plan. When she answered, he told her what had happened.

"Oh, Anthony, you left your phone I think, I found it in the boot of the car after you had gone."

"Sorry, Lids, no, I've got mine with me, in fact I'm phoning you on it!"

They chatted on for a few minutes agreeing to meet at Stansted the following evening. He told his sister that he would ring her from the airport if the plane was delayed. She was easy to talk to; she reminded him so much of someone he knew, someone he hadn't seen for a very long time: his father ... her father. He had never spent as much time thinking of him as he had over the last couple of days. Every time his father's name came up, it was through newspaper articles where he would see his pieces were being exhibited somewhere or other. Laurence Waterman was making a name for himself. Mother dismissed his success as pure luck and refused to discuss him at any length. Anthony respected her in that domain as he knew how hard his mother had found things when she had found herself on her own.

*

"Oh, all right, it must be ... ," my voice faltered.

So it wasn't Anthony's phone. Those same uneasy

feelings were creeping all over me and gathering momentum. Like waves sliding relentlessly across a beach. No way of stopping them either. So the phone had to belong to Douglas; it had been in the dustbin bag with those keys and the wallet. It had fallen out onto the floor of the car boot when I had tipped out his belongings. So why did he have a cheap phone and another set of keys for the flat? I was thinking of all this while half listening to Anthony. He was sounding upset about having missed Father. I couldn't feel much for Father at present. I would think about that later too.

As soon as I had put the receiver down, I reached into my bag. There it was, that little phone. I took it out and flipped it open. It was still switched on and the screen illuminated. I stared at it. Finally, after what seemed like an age, rather than turn it off, and put it back in the bag, I did what most people would have done first. As a naughty child might have done, out of sheer curiosity, I opened the menu, then clicked on address book. There were only two numbers listed. I recognised neither of them. One had just CMP on the name list and the other CL; if these were initials of people, I didn't know them, they didn't mean anything at all to me. I wondered if I should call them but I decided against it. I still wasn't absolutely certain that this was Douglas's phone, although I couldn't think whose else it could have been. Next I checked calls made: none listed. Then I went into the menu for messages received: "Yes", and below it another one "No, 11.30 Mon?". This was so weird. Cryptic messages? I opened the messages sent menu next. There were lots in there, each very similar to the next: 2pm Tues, 4pm Wed, etc. I looked at the dates, and found that they went back over two years. Sometimes there were two in a week, and then there were gaps of a month or so. All were during the day, on weekdays and they had all been sent to CMP. Some more recent ones had slightly different messages: "6pm ring twice, 8pm ring twice." These messages had mostly evening times and they had been sent to CL. So CMP and CL were meeting up with someone, was it Douglas? If this was his phone, then they were things I didn't know about him.

What was he doing? I had never for one second doubted him or felt even a twinge of suspicion about what he did, or where he went. Douglas's love for me was total, all-consuming, passionate. He adored me, of that I was totally certain but it was in an increasingly suffocating way. I felt that now, although I had adored it at the start of the relationship. I had felt wanted, needed and valued. But over the years the pleasure of being owned totally had waned; I was his prisoner, his Rapunzel, the princess locked in the tower so that no-one could ever see me and take me away from him. I had accepted all this because deep down I was afraid of him and so desperate to be loved. I had no idea how to escape either, until Saturday.

Being brutally honest too, was I always totally unhappy? No. But the happiness I felt was based on all the wrong foundations; he was out a lot so I had relative freedom. I had also perfected ways of always being prepared for him when he did come home. He had started to get home later recently. He said there was more pressure on him at work but he always rang and said when he was running late. That would be followed by question after question, where was I, and would I make sure I was home, and dinner ready, because he loved me so much and would make it up to me when he came in.

I had no idea what he did during the day. Well, I knew he was at school, and that he had meetings at the council offices or in other schools or with parents and that he often had to visit other primary schools in the area. There were his lectures and his research for them which took him away too; he talked about all that when he was home. I had never once stopped to think about the veracity of his remarks.

Now I was confronted with a strange situation. I thought about things and wondered if they had made a mistake at the hospital. Perhaps the phone and the keys belonged to someone else. There was something distinctly odd about it all but I really didn't understand how I could find out. Other than phoning those two numbers. I was too afraid to do it though. But it was the only option open to me. If it were his phone, then why on earth would he have it? I summoned up courage, and pressed the dial button to CMP. It started to ring. After four rings it was still unanswered and I lost my nerve and snapped the phone shut. I put it back into my bag.

I had lots to do before I went up to the hospital. I picked up the mail and flicked through the letters. This was the very first time I had done this. Douglas had a thing about it, like he had a thing about so many points. He insisted on opening the mail himself and passed the opened letters to me if he judged I should read them so I never saw most of the mail we received. I looked at each letter carefully, enjoying the opening of them, relishing the reading of them, bills, bank statements, junk mail. I sat at the table reading as if eating a forbidden ice-cream, smoothing down the opened envelopes into a neat little pile.

When I had finished reading the mail, just as would a child, I thought of what else was forbidden fruit, what other things I was not allowed to see. The safe in the bedroom came into my mind; this was another forbidden area in the apartment. Douglas told me that all his plans for my gifts were in there. He kept the passports and both wills there too. I had seen that he had other papers with them as I had walked passed him when he was opening it. I took furtive glances behind his back. The code for the safe was one of his secrets. It had never occurred to me to really want to open the safe. I knew it was out of bounds to me and that was an inevitable that. I never crossed Douglas by requesting anything that he guarded secret. That way I was able to minimise the possibility of making him angry. As I walked towards the bedroom, I thought about that carefully and realised how undermined I was. I just wanted to break the rules for once.

I went through into the bedroom, opened the closet and looked down at the safe. And I was possessed with such a strong desire to disobey that I smiled to myself at the silliness of it all. I knelt on the floor and started to swivel the dial. Six digits, I knew that, I had absently watched Douglas opening it and closing it so very often. Six digits, his date of birth; no, six digits, my date of birth; no, six digits his mother's date of birth. Again and again I tried all the dates I could think of that meant anything to him or to me. Our wedding day, the anniversary of our first meeting ... nothing worked. I stood up, defeated and annoyed and sat down on the bed. Then the credit card wallet which I had found in his trouser pocket came into my mind. I literally ran back into the kitchen and swooped on my handbag, scrabbling for the wallet. Somehow or other, I was absolutely sure that it was Douglas's and that in it I would find the code for the safe. As I drew it out of the handbag I was shaking.

There were four credit cards in the wallet for banks I had no idea he belonged to. There were several bills for hotels we had never stayed in. My mood slowly moved from being questioning and inquisitive to becoming dazed yet indignant. I came across a little card in the wallet which was in my writing, with two sets of six very similar digits: 38 22 34 and below it, written in another hand, in pencil, 38 22 36. My vital statistics! The first set when I had married him and the second last year, when I had been measured for a wedding outfit.

I had written the first set down before I had visited the lady who was making the outfit. The lady had re-measured me and corrected the hip measurement. Douglas, who was with me at the time, had laughed about me having gained two inches around my hips in fifteen years, saying I needed to gain them at the top not there ... and he had pocketed the card and said he would keep it as a souvenir and check on me in fifteen more years.

I strode back to the safe and knew that the first set of digits were the code before I knelt down. Click, click, click, click, click, click and the safe flew open. I looked at the piles of documents in there, then pulled them all out and spread them over the floor. Some were addressed to both of us but a whole separate pile of them were just addressed to Douglas. I opened the top ones. There were bank statements with money in which I knew nothing about, receipts for pieces of jewellery I had never been given, share certificates I did not know existed, dividend receipts, hotel bills. My whole world was falling in around me yet it seemed to me that all I had ever wanted for such a long time was now happening. He had been leading a double life. He had not been honest. I flicked through the pile getting angrier and angrier.

There was a letter with a hospital stamp which took my eye, addressed only to Douglas. This was true forbidden fruit. I took enormous pleasure in taking that one out of its envelope. It had the stamp of a hospital in Lincoln; why on earth he had got mail from a hospital there? He had never been there. As far as I knew. I took the letter out of the envelope and smoothed it out on the floor.

"Dear Mr McIntyre, ... The conclusions of the tests carried out point to the sperm sample provided being of poor quality, ... resulting in the formation of weak embryos ... Damaged DNA can also cause genetic disabilities or birth defects in the baby. If the formation of the embryo is too weak, then miscarriage will occur ... men can have a vital role to play in recurrent miscarriage. It was previously thought to be solely a woman's problem, the causes being either a lack of necessary hormones, cervical weakness or difficulty in implantation but, as your wife has undergone all the necessary tests, it leads us to believe that the cause of Mrs McIntyre's recurrent pregnancy loss may very well be due to poor sperm quality."

He was the reason for all my failures to carry a child to term. I had been told that I was among less than 3% of women who had lost more than three babies but there had never been any mention of the role Douglas had played in the miscarriages. This had been my problem, never in a million years his. I looked again and again at the letter. Suddenly I was thankful at having read it for it took away that terrible guilt I had had for so many, many years. I had wept at each miscarriage, rejoiced at each pregnancy, hoping and hoping that a child would repair our marriage, that a child would make Douglas into the man I dreamed I had married. I was about to put the letter back into the pile and take out another one, when I looked at it once again; I had not noticed the date on it. I took it back out of the envelope and opened it for a second time: 12 February 2004. *Nearly ten years ago. Three months after my second miscarriage.*

This was more than I could bear; his deception was shatteringly vile. There had been no need to go through the pain and loss of those two other poor babies. He knew. He had known and he had kept it from me. He knew that I could never have a child with him. He had lied again. Time seemed to stop as I tried to digest what I had discovered.

Sitting there, I recalled the phone and the bunch of keys. I was certain now that the credit card wallet belonged to Douglas. I went to get my bag and looked closely at the keys. I got my keys and held the two sets together. They were only slightly different. I went to the front door and tried the key on the leather fob. It didn't fit. Then I tried the second key in the patio doors, but that didn't fit either. These were the keys for another apartment. Another apartment? Maybe in the building, Douglas had often said he wanted one day to invest in other property. And there were all those letters to which I had never been privy to reading. Douglas had been covering things up all the time. If he could keep that awful truth about having been the cause of the miscarriages from me, then he could lie about anything at all.

Everything seemed to suddenly fit into place; without another thought, I opened the front door and vaulted up the two flights of stairs to the apartment upstairs. There was tape across the door. I placed the key in the lock and it clicked smoothly and turned. I had known that it would. Had he killed the girl? He was volatile enough to have done it. I shuddered in horror. I could now believe anything of him. I pulled the key back out of the lock and went back downstairs. I wanted now to look at all those papers in the safe but I had to find out what he had done first. And I feared the worst. Despite my fear, I had never felt the delicious sense of freedom that I was experiencing at that moment. By now it was out of the question to go up to the hospital.

I rang the ICU and was told that there was only a slight change. A slight improvement.

"I'll be there in the morning, first thing," I said.

Then a phone call to Mother. I managed to lie convincingly enough about a terrible migraine.

"Mother, I am so sorry, I got back from the airport and lay down on the bed for a snooze, and I only woke up at 4pm. My head is spinning, terrible migraine. Would you mind awfully if I saw you first thing in the morning?"

Mother had no option. I wasn't going to the hospital. I had plans to make before then. We arranged to meet at 10am on Wednesday. I would face the music with her then. From that moment on, I scoured the apartment, made lists of all the monies I knew nothing about, sorted letters into piles. I had information for the police but I needed to do that in my own time, not theirs.

I rang the D.I. and told him I would see him on Thursday. He was very short with me on the phone so I presumed he was with someone.

"No, not tomorrow, Thursday", I repeated.

I packed a small overnight bag ready to leave the apartment the following morning, along with a suitcase crammed with paperwork. This was to be my last night in that place.

*

Jane Waterman sat in the Quiet Room, seething. She had been waiting for almost six hours for Lydia to turn up. She had tried the landline, which was ringing permanently engaged; she had even broken her record and tried Lydia's mobile, which went straight onto the answer phone, and she had wasted two calls doing that already. This was taking things beyond the limit. Lydia must have got back from the airport because Anthony had already rung her from Oslo. He could be counted on to keep in touch, even when he was out of the country, whereas, Lydia, well she had driven less than an hour away from the hospital and had left at 5.30am. She would have got back to the apartment by 8.30 or 9am at the latest and It was now 4pm. Jane had arrived before 10am. And she had been there since, waiting. When eventually Lydia rang around 5 o'clock, it was to tell her that she wasn't even coming today at all.

What happened next in that hospital would live to haunt Jane for a very long time. She had stood up and walked along the corridor, scanning from left to right, wondering how Lydia could possibly dare not to be there; a man walked along the corridor towards her, stopped in front of her, and introduced himself as Detective Inspector Boswell. She mechanically replied that she was Douglas's mother-in-law.

"I'm here to interview Mr McIntyre. We're going to post a policeman outside his room. As soon as he comes round and we're given the go-ahead by the medical team, I'll be interviewing Mr McIntyre."

She was as taken aback as she had been when Laurence had telephoned her to say he was going to settle in the Canaries. Jane was used to being in control and in these two situations, surprise, followed by deep, sustained shock, had got the better of her. She was on the defensive immediately and asked the obvious question,

"What on earth can you possibly want to interview him for?"

"Several things, Madam, but we really need to speak to his wife again first and to inform her... if you will excuse me saying so, you are not his next of kin. I have tried telephoning her but there is no answer and I wouldn't like to leave a message."

"Well, that is all very well but my daughter isn't here.

She has a very severe migraine. So, I am next of kin in her absence and I think you are very rude, Mr Boswell. I have a good mind to telephone your superior, his wife and I play bridge together."

Detective Inspector Boswell stood impassively in front of Jane Waterman. He knew when not to reply. His years as a policeman and as a husband had taught him a thing or two in the psychology stakes. Always count to ten when a woman speaks aggressively to you, that was his motto; it had come from his father, himself a policeman on the Holloway Road. And nine times out of ten it worked. Boswell had often thought of his father's words when his ten-second silence got him out of trouble. Here he was confronted with a potentially volatile situation and he knew he had only one option. Ten seconds. Inevitably after seven seconds, Jane Waterman broke into muffled sobs and sat down defeated. Another non-verbal battle waged and won thanks to Percy Albert Boswell's advice. A true psychologist, an advertisement for advocating common sense instead of years of training. Mark Percy Boswell thought again of his father and inwardly thanked him. He had hated that middle name all through his younger years but now he was proud to own up to it. You definitely cannot put an old head on young shoulders, he thought.

When his phone rang he was still standing in silence in front of Jane. He listened to the call and spoke in monosyllables. Mrs McIntyre was arranging to meet him the day after tomorrow. Jane looked up at him and wondered how he could get away with being so rude.

*

On Wednesday morning the last thing I did before leaving the flat was to play the messages on the answer phone. I deleted every single one just wishing that I could delete the past fifteen years as easily. I walked out of the flat hugely relieved with the large suitcase full of documents, letters and share certificates and an overnight bag. I went up to the hospital, hurrying through the building, dreading the meeting with Mother. She was already seated in the corridor, red in the face, which always meant that she was as angry as hell.

When her eyes fell upon me, there was a dark rage in them, a fury which made me nervous as I got nearer and nearer to her. I had always been as afraid of Mother's rages, almost as much as I was of Douglas's, for different reasons obviously but the effect was largely the same. I had remained crushed by the two people I spent the majority of my time with. I wasn't weak, just unable to fight their behaviour. It was capitulation, but they would never, neither of them, destroy my thoughts, my inner sanctum.

"Excuse me, would you mind if I have a word in private with your daughter?"

*

There was an authority in James Philpott's voice. Jane decided that she would tell Lydia afterwards what she thought of him and she would certainly have a word with Miriam Coles at the Bridge Club. This man needed a lesson in politeness even if he was a good surgeon. She announced that she was going for a breath of air. She stalked out of the hospital, almost banging heads with Celia Philpott in the entrance foyer. Mrs Philpott had looked through her as if she were a ghost. James Philpott must have talked to her about Douglas, she was sure of that. But Celia cut her dead, just staring right through Jane, either making out that she didn't know her or as if she was in total shock and could not muster up enough courage to look at her. She would mention it to Miriam Coles when she next saw her at the Bridge Club. The absolute nerve of the woman, ignoring an older woman, and one whom she knew was going through so much heartache. She reformed her opinion on Celia at that instant and resolved to tell everyone how insulted she had felt.

As she walked around outside, Jane wondered time

and time again what would happen next. Jane had a dark secret. She had truly loved Douglas since the moment she met him; loved him with all her heart and soul from the day Lydia had opened the door to their house and said she had met someone and she wanted her mother to meet him too. Lydia had taken her mother out to the red sports car, because Douglas had told her that he would not come in until her mother had allowed him to cross the threshold. Jane had seen him for that first time and fallen in love with him before he stepped out of the car. He had taken her into his strong sinewy arms and kissed her hand lightly, just as a knight in shining armour might have done. Jane was captivated by him. He could do no wrong in her eyes. She was under his spell.

She loved him secretly as a wife should, not a mother-in-law, and she had borne the disappointment of not becoming a grandmother with little problem. She hated babies of any description anyway and the idea of Douglas being the father of her grandchild did not enchant her in the least. The mere idea was abhorrent to her. So the years had gone by and Jane had loved him from afar. It had strained her relationship with Lydia, but she was proud of the fact that she had kept her feelings to herself and that no-one, not even Douglas had the faintest idea of how she felt.

She knew he was married to Lydia but she felt that he would have been happier with her. She yearned for him and hated the way Lydia was with him. Theirs was a lukewarm marriage for sure. Jane felt bitter. She had been married to a feckless, weak man and this man, who was her idea of the perfect partner, had been married to her daughter, a woman who had exactly the same character as her father. It was all so unfair.

She looked up at one point and saw Lydia walking across the car park. Odd, she thought, she must have left something in the car. Jane called over to her daughter but Lydia didn't turn around. Jane called louder, but Lydia still didn't look around, in fact she started running.

Mr Philpott looked intently at me as Mother walked away. I could feel him staring at me. Yes, I thought, I do look burned-out, don't I? You are so right, Mr Philpott.

"Mrs McIntyre, your husband has regained consciousness and is asking for you; would you come this way, please?" said Mr Philpott. "I would ask you to be brief for this first time. Remember, he has just regained consciousness."

I went towards the ICU, past the police officer, gowned up quickly and softly opened the door to Douglas's room. As I looked down at him, he opened his eyes and smiled at me, starting to move his tubed hand towards me. He closed his eyes as if in gratefulness, as if pleased I was there. I looked down stonily at the closed eyes. I realised so perfectly that I could move forward. I would not go back to the limbo I had been in for years. I didn't need to kill this man, for he was already dead in my eyes. He had maybe killed that poor girl in the flat upstairs. He had as good as snuffed out any life in me too. He deserved everything that was coming to him.

There has to be a defining moment in every person's life, when the past becomes a nasty blur and the present is something to be embraced as the gift it really is. I was there looking down at the man who had consumed me, body and soul, for over sixteen years. I felt nothing but pure elation at seeing his broken body. I cared not whether he was well or ill, I knew that from here on, what counted for me was *me*, and that I would move on today, without him. I stood there and knew that I would soon be walking out of that hospital for the last time. I turned away from him and softly closed the door, knowing that I was opening another door to my own life as an independent woman. I hastily took off the mask, the gown, the protective shoe bags and threw them into a basket. I had wasted enough time, there was not a second now that did not count for me. I would not spend one more in his presence.

"Mrs McIntyre, would you mind stepping into my office please?" said James Philpott, whom I suddenly found to be walking beside me as I strode down the corridor. I slowed my pace, out of politeness, then turned to face him. I looked carefully at him.

"No, Mr Philpott, I will not. I suggest you telephone Heather McIntyre. She is Mr McIntyre's next of kin and lives in New Zealand. I have her number but not with me, and I neither have the time nor inclination to get it. You will be able to get it by telephoning my mother."

I hastily scribbled Mother's mobile number on to a scrap of paper and pushed it into James Philpott's palm. I left him standing in the corridor with his hand still outstretched; I walked off, turned the corner and summoned the lift. I looked about at the motley group of patients and visitors in there, on their way in and out of the building. Silence, just the sound of compressed air as the lift disgorged people and swallowed them alternately. I finally got out at the main entrance. As the doors closed behind me to move other bodies up and down, I slung my bag over my shoulder and walked out of the building.

*

The surgeon stood there shocked, in mute astonishment. He had never witnessed any relative reacting like this. He had seen spouses racked with grief, prostrate in tears, in fits of temper and in black rage. He had dealt with all that and he had been able to pass on his sympathy and his caring attitude to all those he came into contact with. But this was different. He had seen for the last few days at home that life was full of surprises, but today his professional one broke new ground too.

Douglas opened his eyes for a fraction of a second and saw Lydia. He was so grateful that she was there. He closed them again; he was so tired, tired as hell, but glad she was there, relieved. He moved his hand across the sheet to hold hers. But he only found the edge of the bed. His fingers spidered across between the sheets and tubes. When he finally opened his eyes again to behold his wife, she was no longer there. Had she been there at all? He waited and waited falling in and out of slumber. He recalled being moved around, being rocked slightly. He had no idea whether minutes, hours, days or weeks had passed.

*

Lydia Waterman is my name once more from today onwards. My thoughts turn to this first day of the rest of my life, no longer my life in Douglas's wake or in Mother's shadow: mine, my very own. I am not going to the airport to pick Anthony. Tomorrow I'll go down to the police station and make a formal statement. I'll hand over the phone, the keys, the wallet, the letters. I'll tell them that those keys fitted the girl's flat. As I walk towards the car, I hear Mother's cries across the car park. And I keep on walking then break into a brisk trot until Mother's cries become fainter and fainter. My first little triumph.

*

Jane stood there stupefied. That daughter of hers had only just arrived! As she wondered what was happening, her phone began to ring. It was Mr Philpott asking for Heather's number. He wouldn't be drawn on why, Jane asked him what was happening, but he flatly refused to enlighten her, he just told her to ask her daughter. Her daughter had just left the hospital, she told him. Did he know where she was going? Jane was trying the old twenty question technique with James Philpott but he was used to dealing with people like her. He very politely told her his other phone was bleeping and said he would have to go. Jane Waterman stood there totally baffled. She was infuriated but worried that things had worsened for Douglas. What other reason would the doctor have for phoning his sister?

SIX

Oslo held no charm for Anthony any longer as he walked out of the Kongresscenter. All he had wanted to do was to meet his father. This trip back to the UK had made him think. Here he was, a successful businessman, 31, no ties, but no ties meant no links. The two words didn't mean the same, ties could not be undone without loosening something. Links were part of a chain, part of a whole, part of a family, and Anthony knew now that he needed those links which had been broken when he was a teenager.

He walked around the centre of Oslo aimlessly. There had been no reason for Anthony to think that Laurence did not care. After all, his father was an artist, and he had had a partner and her child to support for many years now. He sat at a café table and phoned his father's number. It rang out and then the answer phone kicked in, first in Spanish, then in English,

"Hello, thanks for phoning Laurence Waterman who is not available. He will call you back if you care to leave your name, number and the motive for your call after the tone."

"Hi Dad, just thought I would try and touch base with you, I went to Norway to see you but..."

Anthony's voice trailed off, and when he was invited to register his message or cancel it, he opted to cancel and clicked his phone off. No, he needed to *see his father*. Leaving a message was too silly after all this time. He spent the rest of the day catching up on business calls, and visited a couple of art galleries in the late afternoon before going back to his hotel and ordering a sandwich with room service. He was asleep by 9pm.

On Wednesday morning he took a taxi to the airport and bought an earlier flight back. He rang Lydia and left her a message, telling her he would hire a car from the airport and see her at the hospital in the afternoon. Anthony regretted those lost links for the very first time in his life. He had never tried to get in touch with Laurence. Maybe, some of what his mother had told them wasn't true? He started to have his doubts as he sat on the plane. He resolved to bring up the subject with Lydia as soon as he saw her. As he got out of the airport, he checked his phone. Lydia had left three messages. The first one, to thank him for letting her know about the re-arranged flight, the second one to say she was going away till Thursday and the third one, a couple of minutes after the second to say she was leaving Douglas.

Anthony listened to the three messages again and again before he drove away. Lydia sounded so calm. She could have been telling him she had just ordered a pizza. As he listened the phone started to ring. It was his mother, frantic. He pulled the car over to the hard shoulder and listened as his mother explained in between wails, what had happened since he had left. Douglas had regained consciousness. Lydia had been in to see Douglas and taken fright, run away from the hospital and was nowhere to be found. She had left without a word to anyone. Douglas was going to be interviewed by the police, and she couldn't understand what was going on at all. The only thing she knew for certain was that Lydia was nothing like her and that she felt like she could never speak to her again. The wailing went on and on; finally Anthony said he had no battery left in his phone. As he switched the phone to mute, he realised that his mother had no idea that he was back in the country. She wasn't expecting him until very late that night. With that he resumed his drive to the hospital. The hospital. He slowed down again and pulled in.

"Hello Lids, I've decided to come down to Cambridge too. Don't worry if you don't want to talk."

*

I had returned to Cambridge to exorcise the man who had bewitched me there in those gardens. The person who had kept me a virtual prisoner all these years. What an utter fool I had been! So many years wasted and time was more important than any sum of money, any property, any man. Duped and deceived. I had lived with a brutal, cheat of a man; I had grown up today. I sat on the same bench in those same College gardens and thought of the last few days. I had come back here to put an end to what had started in this very garden. Finish it in my mind as well as physically, place it behind me, part of my past. I knew for certain that Douglas was involved with the woman upstairs. I pulled that little red phone out of my bag and looked at it again. CL was her, Claire Leaver, of course, D.I. Boswell had told me the woman's name. The keyring had an initial C too. I wondered if Douglas had been on this phone at the time of the crash; that would explain him swerving at the last second.

I opened up the phone and went into the menu. Silly I thought, I already checked the phone the other day and there were only two names in the sent list. And one of them was dead. Then it came to me, to look in drafts. If he was texting when he crashed, then of course he didn't have the chance to send the message. Simple. Why did I not think of that before? Drafts : there it was. Written at 2.20 pm, Saturday April 13, it was there waiting, unsent, to CMP. He had killed one woman and then got in his car to meet the other. CMP. I opened it. "Plough Inn, 3pm?" How incredibly sordid. I thought it through. He had no doubt engineered the argument because he wanted to get out of the house and see this woman. He had left the flat on purpose to meet her. He was having an affair with two other women at the same time. I had never once thought of him being unfaithful. I had trusted him, had blindly worshipped him. How utterly disgusting it seemed now.

I had naïvely thought that he was besotted with me and me alone. And now there was proof of two women, one of whom was dead. Who then was this other?

I began to understand why Douglas had so often been delayed, or had had to go back to work, or needed to go and play a quick round of golf to "clear his mind", "to loosen up", as he put it. I wanted to yell at the top of my voice, smash my fists into a wall. I regretted every single second that I had devoted to this bullying, masochistic , adulterous man. I was so very glad it had all come to an end. Every excuse he had ever made for leaving the flat had been a complete and utter lie. He had so often come home from those sorties and taken me to bed. I put the phone down onto the bench, got up and vomited into the bushes behind me.

Two women, one dead. The one way to find out was to ring that number. I remembered that I had actually rung the number yesterday and it had rung out. I took the phone up from the bench, looked up the number and copied it onto a slip of paper. Then I took my own phone out and tapped it in. It rang out once more. I was shaking as a voice cut in quickly.

"Celia Philpott speaking."

I held my breath, closed my eyes and in the space of a few terrible seconds thought very very fast. Of course. I was no longer shocked at anything regarding Douglas, I was finished with him. I did not care.

"Hello, who is this?"

"This is Lydia, Lydia McIntyre. I am returning your call regarding Mr McIntyre's health."

I had just realised that Celia Philpott would not be aware that I even knew about Douglas's second phone. She had phoned me the other day asking how Douglas was. Now I understood why. How sick it all was! Celia Philpott, the wife of the man who had saved Douglas's life and the mother of a little boy who had been at Douglas's school. Celia Philpott had it all and yet she had wanted more. Well she could have it.

"Oh, hello Mrs McIntyre, thank you for phoning, have you any better news..."

"No need to thank me. News, yes, better, I'm not so sure. You have been seeing my husband for the last two years. You should have been meeting him on Saturday at 3pm but he didn't get chance to send his text. He crashed into a wall as he was sending it. Ironic isn't it, you are the reason he is in the ICU now. And have you for one minute thought who saved his life in the hospital? Ah, I just read your thoughts. You got it in one, and your husband was operating on him at the time you should have been screwing him. Strange twist of fate that. Wait till Mr Philpott finds out that he saved his wife's lover's life. By the way, I said my husband, I should have said my *ex*-husband. And as you appear to go in for second-hand soiled goods, please feel free, he's all yours now, you can't wait I bet, no need for furtive behaviour. You might want to pack a bag or two first and try and organise a place to stay for the night until you manage to rent somewhere because if your husband is anything like me, he will throw you straight out. Oh, I clean forgot you are a bit like myself in only one way. You are also a kept woman? Now you will need to sort out a little nest egg from somewhere, because I can promise you one thing, darling Douglas won't have a shirt to his back never mind a bank account to fall back on once he gets out of hospital... if he ever does, of course."

Celia sobbed, pleading with me to stop, but I did not stop. I told her everything, from the secret bank accounts, the secret gifts, his drinking, the ill-treatment, the miscarriages, the lies, the girl in the flat upstairs, the fact that she was not the only fish in Douglas's murky, tempest-tossed sea. Within five minutes I had painted the Machiavellian portrait that was the real Douglas McIntyre and Celia was a gibbering wreck. Then the phone had cut out. It didn't matter to me. I had nothing more to say.

*

Celia had been standing at her kitchen sink when her phone rang in her apron pocket. She had listened in shock to Lydia, like a person watching a horror movie or a thriller, who just really needs to turn the damn thing off rather than be frightened witless. Celia was unable to put the phone down, unable to bring herself to blank this ranting woman. Then she summoned up her nerve and did just that. She threw the phone into the washing -up bowl she was standing over. She ran over to the wall socket and wrenched the landline out of its housing. As she stood there, holding the flex, she knew she now had few options left open to her. She would have to tell James, admit everything. She had to try and save her marriage. She thought frantically of Fergus returning from Scout Camp in two days' time, and of what her week had turned into. She had to do it tonight, she had to make things right between herself and James. Nothing was worth losing him, she had to try and put the past, and this awful week firmly behind her. Her resolve was not so solid though, because she was in too much a state of shock for that .

Could all of what she had just heard be true? She had risked everything for this. There was nothing else to be done than to tell James, and tonight. Her whole body shook at the thought of it. But Fergus would be back on Friday. From that moment on she did nothing at all but think of how she could tell James. She paced about nervously. She couldn't think straight, she had no idea how to begin to tell him and she had no idea either how he would react. She thought she knew him, but waiting like this, she realised that she had not a clue what he might do or say. It was beyond her. She knew that she had been such a fool.

Jane Waterman drove home in a worried state and searched in her address book for Heather's number, scribbled it down onto a notepad and pushed the pad into her handbag. She ran back out to her car and retraced her way back to the hospital. She paced up and down the corridor. She had been down to the restaurant and had a coffee, gone into the hospital shop and met an old friend from Bridge Club who had asked after Douglas; Dorothy Gregg was the woman's neighbour and had told her how serious it was. Everyone felt so sorry for Lydia. Jane reacted as if the name had stung her. There was all this to face as well, and everyone in the town would soon know about it. Jane was an inveterate snob; her world of gossip about others had just turned full circle onto her and she was about to become the most talked-about person in the area, and for all the wrong reasons. She didn't know the half yet.

She just could not understand what was going on. Lydia was being her old evasive self, had disappeared into thin air and when Jane had gone back up to the ICU, she had been told that they would shortly be moving Douglas out to a private room on an orthopaedic ward. She assumed that Lydia would be back soon to go with him only to be told that Mrs McIntyre had left the hospital and that they had no idea where she was. Maybe she was over at the other ward by now, volunteered one of the ward orderlies. So Jane knew that Lydia had not come back here after she had seen her running across the car park a couple of hours earlier. Then that odious fat little detective had come into the corridor and looked at her, looked about and around her as if he was going to ask her something, then he had walked up to her, and straight past her without so much as a nod of the head or a comment. This was all too much, Lydia has hardly been here at all, thought Jane. She was hurt, hurt for Douglas. There had been no other thought in her mind since Saturday than him. It was now Wednesday. These five days had been complete torment.

She did not understand why Anthony had come all this way and then jetted off suddenly to Norway...of all places. She secretly wondered if it was to meet up with a girlfriend. Girls had come and gone in Anthony's life but no-one had stayed longer than a few months. Just as she was wondering all this, her phone bleeped. She was sure it would be a text message from Lydia with yet another excuse and an apology.

It was Anthony; he was back early and was going down to Cambridge. Cambridge? Jane read the text and was puzzled. She had spoken to him this morning but she had thought he was still in Oslo. For once she did not stop to think about what the call would cost her.

"Anthony, what is going on, why are you going to Cambridge and have you any idea where Lydia is? What could she be doing, when her place is here? She has been gone since yesterday. What on earth is she thinking of?"

That was four questions rattled off, an average for Jane.

"They are moving Douglas and he is asking for her. The police are here too."

"Mother, you will have to speak to her yourself, this is nothing to do with me. Look I am driving, and my battery is bleeping again."

And he rang off. Jane was beside herself with rage, first at having been cut off, but secondly and more annoyingly, at not having solved the mystery of Lydia's whereabouts. There was also an element of disquiet moving through her and affecting her demeanour. She had no idea why she felt like that. She was starting to feel worried. Douglas was going to be interviewed by the police; an officer was outside his room. This was surely not because of a banal traffic accident, where no-one except Douglas himself had been injured.

What had he been doing last Saturday afternoon? She sat in the corridor turning over her thoughts, then spied Mr Philpott coming towards her. He looked up, spotted her, smiled awkwardly, then turned on his heel and walked away quickly in the opposite direction. Jane didn't have time to even call out his name.

Jane became even more concerned but her anger got the better of her. He had just ignored her! And his wife had done the same this morning! She started to get up, then sat down, then got up again and looked around her, willing a solution to pop out from somewhere, anywhere. She was totally alone here, and she did not like it. She had no idea at all what she could do. She turned the mobile over and over in her hand, willing it to ring. How different her attitude about the device was to what her normal everyday one was! She decided to ring Lydia once again. As she dialled, she wondered whether Lydia might have had an accident. This was the first time she had actually worried about her daughter. Answer phone again. Just a glimmer of anxiousness began to form in her mind; she began to wonder too if that were the case, how would they know where *she*, her mother, was? Would they have made the connection with Douglas's name? What if she weren't in the same hospital? But this was all hypothetical. Wild thoughts, stupid of her. Of course there had to be a perfectly sensible and reasonable solution.

At that point, her thoughts ran back to Douglas, she decided to follow the directions to the orthopaedic ward and ask if she could go in to see him. At least that was a logical thing to do, instead of waiting here. As she started the long walk over to the new wing, she became suddenly calmer. She knew why there was this silence from her daughter. Lydia's phone was turned off. She just had to be in the hospital and you weren't supposed to use them in the hospital although she had seen lots of people doing so. Jane had always instilled the need to respect rules in her children and she consoled herself now with the fact that to a large extent she had been successful, since she had managed their teenage years single-handed. Both of them were well brought-up, sound individuals, despite Laurence's bohemian streak. That had not rubbed off on either of her children, thank God. Lydia was one for following rules and regulations. She had lots of Laurence's faults but she was not one to break the hospital code. Jane brushed away the fact that *she* had just broken those rules.

She pondered sullenly as she walked. She would get to the orthopaedic ward and there they would be together and once more, like each time, she would have that raw feeling of resentment and distaste when she saw them as a couple. Lydia was not there. Jane walked over to the nurses' station and was directed to a private room. No, Mr McIntyre had been asking for his wife but as yet she hadn't been in to the orthopaedic ward. Jane listened to the nurse and felt some relief. She could go in and see Douglas alone. She forgot her anxiety for an instant but then it came over her like a wave engulfing her as she looked ahead. Approaching the door, she became full of foreboding. There was a policeman standing there, arms folded, staring into space.

As Laurence Waterman came out of Fuerteventura airport Hakim ran over joyfully to him and hugged him. Laurence felt the thrill of being wanted and cherished. He was home and glad to be there. He was filled with happiness to see Hakim. He put a reassuring arm around the boy's shoulder and strode across the concourse towards Naseera.

"So good to see you Laurence, but you should have stayed that extra day and taken advantage of being in Oslo. We have had dozens of e-mails about the exhibition and lots of offers of work coming in. We'll need an army of labourers to cope with the demand!!"

Naseera laughed as she said this, Laurence would never employ anyone to churn out copies of his works, expansion in that sense for him was a no-no, his thoughts were not at all turned to making a quick fortune. It smacked of commercialism and he was an artist, not a salesman. You only had to drive along the main arteries of the island to see the fruits of commercialism. Garden Centres were everywhere selling pots by the dozen and every single one of them a factory churned out masterpiece from some Chinese sweatshop. Laurence knew that this bread and butter pottery bore no resemblance to his artwork but to a lot of people pottery was pottery. Ceramic artists like himself compared with industrial artists was like comparing

MacDonald's to Michel Blanc. Laurence felt so lucky to be doing a job he loved and getting paid for it.

Both he and Naseera were on the same wave length. She teased him about his lack of business acumen and he teased her about twittering on to him and wanting to turn his workshop into a factory. They were a symbiotic couple. Each knew the other's limits and respected them. A married couple could not have had more regard for each other than they had. There was a warmth between them which was palpable. Laurence felt it keenly, often sighed thankfully at that fateful exhibition success in Tunis all those years before. He had lived since then, at least re-lived the happiness he had had when his own two children had been growing up.

When the odd trio had arrived back at the house, Laurence brought out his gifts for them. For Hakim there was a new watch, and for Naseera a pretty set of candles which the Norwegians are so clever at producing. Each of them sat around the table recounting their time apart. The phone call from Anthony was mentioned and Laurence listened intently.

Laurence had explained many times to Naseera that he had lost so much when he left his family in the UK; she had listened to him, but had known that this part of his life was unknown, uncharted territory for her. She never pressed him to talk about it, she knew he had regrets but those regrets were his and his alone. She knew too that Hakim and herself had in some way filled the gap he had in his life but yet she did not feel that she had replaced anyone. She had her grief at losing her own family. She had taken hold of Hakim and walked out of the house down to the market, complaining from behind to her mother standing in the doorway as she left. She was angry at having always to look after the little one, because she was the eldest in the family. She was sulking, whilst her other brothers got on with their own lives. She felt the injustice keenly. She wanted more out of her life than to move from baby-sitter to wife. Her parents already had plans for her in that direction.

Within minutes of leaving, their flimsy apartment block was blown apart. The three-storey building had dominoed down with thunderous groans. Naseera ran for cover out of instinct, thinking the world had come to an end, shielding Hakim under her, he the terrified five-year-old, she the big, grown-up sister of sixteen. Their world did end that day. They spent the next few days in a makeshift tent. Neighbours lent them clothes, and Naseera watched in silent horror as the rescue workers pulled out one lifeless body after another from the ruins of the building she had called home.

And here she was in another home, another life so far removed from the previous one as to be unable to make any comparisons. Six years ago Laurence had walked into her life, because of Hakim. She had a lot to thank her little brother for. That day in El Djem had changed all their lives. When she got the letter from Laurence a few weeks later, she read it and re-read it. She was so afraid that what he really wanted was a wife. She could not love the man as a husband. She did not want that, no matter how good it might have been for Hakim. Yet she was torn too because she knew that his offer meant a new beginning for her little brother. She did not consider what the offer would mean to her, because she was so sure that nothing could ever come right in her life now. She felt that she had cheated death; in some way she had been given that second chance that four members of her family had not.

Her aunt and uncle were wonderful to her. They offered to house Laurence for a month until she had made up her mind. Laurence made things clear straight away to them but still Naseera was not convinced. No, he didn't want a wife, no he didn't want a lover, no he didn't want a housekeeper. He just wanted to give something back, to share his good fortune and to feel as if he was needed in some way. Meeting a person who possesses such a streak of pure selflessness is strange and rare in anyone's life. It was unbelievable to Naseera.

He explained his situation to her and she translated for her aunt and uncle. He insisted to all of them that he did not want them to think he was trying to assuage any guilt or failure that he may have acquired as a parent himself. He was thinking of himself too. He felt that he could change all their lives for the better.

They all sat around the table and worked out a plan. Hakim pulled at Laurence's arm and took him onto the little balcony and showed him his collection of cars. Naseera felt that Hakim liked this man, she sensed his seal of approval. Finally Naseera agreed to go back with Laurence and it was he who insisted on there being a trial period, for all their sakes. So the plan emerged: Naseera and Hakim would go back to Fuerteventura for a month, and that first month was extended to six then suddenly, here they all were, six years later. Naseera didn't feel grateful to Laurence. It all seemed so natural, so right. She did however feel sincere affection for him. She felt too that he had been good for her brother, and that although he had lost growing up in his own country, he had taken on another culture and a whole host of values which had set him on the road of life with more chances than if he had stayed in Tunis. She too had gained a lot from this new life. She pushed out of her mind what her parents would have thought. That was pointless, those kind of thoughts meant nothing, did not lead you forward, did not help you in any way at all. That was her former existence, this was her present one. And ne'er the twain shall meet, which was one of Laurence's phrases that fitted her mood perfectly. She was finding it harder and harder to imagine what her life in Tunis would have been like, if only, if only ...

"I wonder what Anthony wanted? It has been so long since we spoke," said Laurence.

Anthony had turned the phone off and was driving along the M11; he would be in Cambridge in less than 40 minutes. What a few days this was turning out to be! He was going to see his sister and spend some time with her. He had tried to see his father and failed. He had been summoned over by his mother and had not yet even seen Douglas. Not that important a detail, maybe now, he mused, thinking over the phone message from Lydia.

As he drove into Cambridge, he rang his sister. She asked him to meet her in the Orchard of Jesus College and told his she had booked two single rooms for the night in the College. When Anthony arrived he drove up to the entrance on Victoria Avenue and went through the electronic gates.

Jesus College was founded in 1496 on the site and buildings of the twelfth-century Benedictine convent of St Mary and St Radegund. The nuns' church is still used as the college Chapel. Anthony was pleased to be back there where he remembered visiting his sister, but then Douglas had appeared on the scene and Lydia moved into another circle of which Anthony was no longer a part.

When his turn had come to apply for university, he went further afield; to the great pride of his mother, he won a scholarship to Reading University studying for a BSc in Nutrition with Food Consumer Sciences. After completing his degree and gaining a first, he walked into an MPhil in Nutritional Sciences at King's College London. He had rarely been home after leaving for Reading and once he was in London, the ties to home loosened further. He never went back there to live.

He asked for directions to the Orchard and quickly spotted Lydia sitting on a bench. As he was walking over to her, she looked up and smiled, stood up and walked towards him. This was their second meeting in as many days, after years and years apart. Anthony folded his arms around her and she clung on to him like a child. No sobbing, no tears just a firm grip around him and silence, such a long silence.

Finally, Lydia stood back from him and asked him to sit down.

"I have a lot to say, Anthony, I need you to listen carefully."

"That's why I'm here, Lids," he said as he sat down next to her.

"You know, Anthony, from the age of 15, I had to put myself second in whatever I did. For four years after Father left, I pandered to Mother's fits of temper, crying episodes - always smoothing her path so that my own life could be less troublesome. Then I married and very soon after I realised that Douglas needed to control me in order for him to be fulfilled in some bizarre way. I have spent my whole life so far, succumbing to the whims and desires of others. I didn't come second, I came third in the pecking order. I have had no life of my own, and yet to all around me I had everything I wanted. Douglas dominated me from the first day we met on this very bench. I loved him totally and without measure."

"Oh, Lids, but ....."

"No, Anthony, please don't interrupt me just yet, I need to say this. I need you to listen. It is actually helping me to tell you. At the back of my mind, I saw marriage to him as the ideal I had always dreamed of but instead of that and within months, I was ill-treated both physically and mentally. Frequently. Time after time. I did not deserve it, I was weak I know, but weakness is not a failing. I was powerless because he imposed his strength and crushed my individuality. You know, I really showed that I had individuality at work. I was admired by my colleagues and I was promoted. I had a good reputation as a landscape architect. I let it all go to have Douglas's child, on Douglas's terms. Anthony, believe me, when I gave in my notice I was summoned to see the Managing Director and he asked me, he almost pleaded with me to reconsider. He told me that I had a promising career. I so very much wanted to tell him that I was sure I could run a family and a home and have a job that I loved too, but I stood there in front of him and spoke Douglas's words instead. I said, 'I am sure that it would be totally impossible to combine bringing up a child or children and running a home and giving 100% to my job here.' I was so afraid of asserting myself that doing so was no longer an option or even a remote possibility. Douglas was violent to me when I was a mouse, Douglas could have killed me if I became a lion. Anthony, I realise that I've been so very foolish. Now is the time to make changes. I think I should tell you too that Douglas has been unfaithful, for how long I don't know."

*

Anthony looked sideways at me.

"Our financial affairs are a complete mystery to me. He has been squirrelling away money for some time, maybe ever since I have been married to him. Not only that but he is somehow or other mixed up in the murder which took place in our apartment block last Saturday, the day of his accident. He has been lying to me for years, Anthony, and I have accepted everything he said as the truth. None of it was so. Plus he has abused me both physically and verbally for many years too."

I looked down at the ground. Anthony shifted his position on the bench, awkward and embarrassed at seeing me so bereft.

"I had decided that I had had enough after the last episode, which was ... last Saturday..."

At which point I lifted the hair from my face and neck to reveal a nasty bruise on my temple and the long red weal along my neck towards my shoulder.

"... on Saturday afternoon, but then there was the crash and then I found out ... other things."

I lifted my eyes towards the sky, as if looking for some divine intervention to take away all the pain.

Anthony was both stunned and furious.

"No one deserves this, Lydia have you never for one instant let anyone know what was going on"? He put his arm around me and stroked my hair.

"Thank goodness, given this horrendous situation, that you have no children to consider, Lydia."

I crumpled before him and he knew he had committed a

grave error. Too late, no way one can take back the words, he thought. If only, if only... It is true though that there is nothing that anyone can say in such circumstances that will not offend or cause suffering in some way or other. Some people prefer to keep silent in situations. That can be wrongly interpreted too.

"I lost four babies Anthony. I was racked with guilt at being unable to give Douglas the child he said he wanted. I saw it as my failure, when in fact it was his. I became a full-time housewife, waiting on his every need, being there for him every waking moment. He even checked the mileage on my car, my phone record on the monthly bill, my cheque book stubs, my credit card statements. I had to ring him at lunchtime, otherwise he would come home raging that I had forgotten. It was easier for me to check in at lunchtime than to suffer the consequences of that temper."

I could see that Anthony felt sorry for me. He was the very first person to actually find out the real truth. He could never have dreamed that it was as bad as this.

We sat together for a long time, not speaking at all, just together, time between us ticking by, people ambling past, a distant clock chiming, no words needed. The peace of the place helped to calm us both. This old nunnery had been standing for almost a thousand years, our existence here was a mere speck of ink on the reams of parchment that had been written in this place.

"Thanks for coming, Anthony, and please don't worry if you think that you have said the wrong thing. I am fragile at present, but I will be OK. At least I am free now; and the wasted years are behind me. There is no sense in looking back now. I made my own mistakes, now I have to learn from them. I have to get through the task of telling Mother."

"I'll tell her," he said firmly.

"I can't think about that now. Do tell me about Father, how is he, what did you do in Oslo? Dear me, I sound like Mother, twenty questions! Go on, tell me all about it."

So Anthony explained to me about his unsuccessful trip to Oslo and how he had gone into the Kongresscenter so full of hope and pride only to realise that he had missed his father, that he had got the days mixed up and that his father had in fact left his hotel early and gone back to the Canaries via Madrid.

"He'll be arriving there today, as far as I know. But, you know Lydia, I have made up my mind, I am going to go and see him there. I really want to see him again. I think it is only fair for me to make an effort now, although I really have no need at all to do so. Father must have just had quite enough of trying to suit Mother and felt like he needed to be himself again. I am sure about that. She must have really cramped his style. So he jacked everything in to make a life of his own."

"Which meant leaving his children to suit himself? Instead of standing by them and waiting until they were off his hands financially? I call that damned selfish, Anthony. Remember how mother had to struggle to pay us through university? And he never once got in touch, apart from coming to my ..."

My voice grew weaker and I stopped and looked away. I changed the conversation and asked my brother if it were OK for him to stay the night there. I had already booked two single rooms in the College. He agreed and we went together back to his car to pick up his overnight bag, then went up to the rooms overlooking the cricket pitch. There was a little balcony leading out from my room. We talked there for another hour or so. I told him that I had to go to the police the following morning. Anthony suggested that we could go together.

I rang Boswell about the keys fitting the upstairs flat. I also told him that I had the phone that Douglas had maybe been using when the accident happened. And that I knew who he had been phoning. Boswell explained that he would be speaking to Douglas in the morning. The hospital had given him the go-ahead to do a full interview. He arranged to meet me at the police station at 11am.

*

Meanwhile Anthony took on the task of phoning Mother. It proved to be less of a problem than he had anticipated. She had left the hospital before lunchtime and gone home with one of her "turns" and was waiting for her GP to call. In the end, Anthony had no need to tell her anything because she never so much as asked. She was too wrapped up in feeling woozy. Anthony was inwardly extremely grateful for those dizzy spells.

In fact Jane Waterman had spotted that policeman outside Douglas's room and gone straight home to hide. She had made certain though to remember to leave Heather's number with the nurses' station.

SEVEN

James Philpott had spent Wednesday sorting out various problems. He was not operating but had a clinic in the afternoon and had done his ward rounds that morning. He had asked for it to be arranged for Douglas McIntyre to be transferred to an orthopaedic ward; he had seen the man's wife that morning and had been thoroughly taken aback by her reaction. He had witnessed the woman walk away from him, out of the hospital without so much as an explanation. All she had done was flatly refuse to see her husband, and as she was leaving she had given him her mother's mobile phone number and told him to contact her to get Mr McIntyre's next of kin; that she was no longer his next of kin. What a strange set of circumstances, he thought, and how odd that she should choose this moment to leave her husband.

He had managed to ask her mother to let them have the man's sister's address without telling her that Mrs McIntyre had told him to do so. He deftly skirted around her questioning, telling her he had to answer his bleeper, that he knew how understanding she was of his situation. He was used to dealing with potentially explosive incidents.

He had dealt equally swiftly with D.I.Boswell.

He was in the middle of his paperwork when his phone bleeped.

"Yes, Philpott, here."

"Mr Philpott, sorry to bother you. It's Joanne Whalley here, staff nurse on Orthopaedic. I have a Mr McIntyre on the ward, who came down here just this afternoon and who is insisting on speaking to you personally. He has become very agitated; I thought as he was transferred here from your unit that it might be judicious to let you know. I have managed to calm him down a little by telling him I would phone you and ask you if you could spare him a few minutes of your time. I told him that I had no idea if you were still on duty. He has been going on like this for the last couple of hours and won't stop ringing the buzzer to ask if I have spoken to you. Would you mind awfully...?"

"OK, Nurse Whalley, tell him I will call in on him before I leave the hospital. It's 6.30 now, I should be over in the next hour."

James Philpott was beginning to wonder whether he would ever be able to get home early. Every time he thought he would be able to go straight home, something always cropped up. And he was tired out. He had been on call all last weekend, he hadn't slept well since Sunday, because Celia was in such a strange frame of mind. No day was ever the same in his job but at least his home life had been on an even keel. Until last weekend.

Once he had finished the paperwork and checked in on the ICU, he walked over to the new wing. Nurse Whalley approached him as he arrived and took him into Douglas's room.

Douglas sensed that he was being rocked slightly and heard squeaking, wheels squeaking. He was regaining consciousness. There was more light and more noise. A clinking of glass or metal, mumbled, low tones. He opened his eyes and squinted up; he saw a person looking back at him, swathed in bandages, grotesque. He was starting to really focus on the man when suddenly he moved. Douglas realised he was in a lift. The man he had seen was indeed himself in the reflection of the roof. The lift had come to a halt. They were moving him out of it and along a lighter corridor. He could hear people around him, walking towards him, then moving to one side as the trolley he was being pushed along on cut a swathe in the middle of the corridor. Within a few minutes he was in a room. The nurse stood by the bed and checked his pulse and blood pressure, chattering on to him. He stared out of the window, then heard something she said and turned to face her.

"What did you say?" he asked her.

"I said that Mr Philpott is so pleased with your progress. This is what makes our job worthwhile."

Douglas lay very still after she had gone. After a while, he looked around for the buzzer and pressed it.

"Nurse, I need to speak to Mr Philpott, it's very urgent."

Douglas rang that buzzer every five minutes asking to see the consultant.

"Good evening, Mr McIntyre, you wanted to see me?" said James Philpott.

"I need you to know some facts; I tried to end my life on Saturday. You see, I just couldn't carry on any longer. My wife has been seeing someone else. I found out about it quite by accident on Saturday lunchtime. She is trying everything to get out of it, spreading lies about me. Well I'd had enough and I just couldn't bear the thought of carrying on, of people finding out. But now is the time to be frank and to come out with the whole thing and put you in the picture. I want you to know the whole truth. I have lived with the awful facts for weeks and on Saturday, I just decided that I could no longer cope with the shame of it all. My whole career ruined because of her, it was all too much to bear."

Douglas McIntyre stammered over his words and then went silent. James felt uncomfortable. James's own mother had a saying which came back to him as he waited for McIntyre to break the silence. Alice Philpott used to say, "Yes James, but you never know what goes on behind a front door." Homespun philosophies were her forte, she had a saying for every occasion. James knew he had to wait for the man to speak, rather than give him something to reply to.

He edged him nearer a response, rather thinking of trying to bring this meeting to an end. He just wanted to go home.

"Go ahead, then, Mr McIntyre. I am listening."

James Philpott was slightly nervous; he could not see where this conversation could be heading and he started to wonder if Mr McIntyre might be delusional.

"Things came to a head on Saturday lunchtime when I realised that I just could not carry on with all the deception any longer. We had a huge argument about it, and I told her I wanted a divorce. I told her I was leaving her."

"So you want me to know this, but quite frankly, where do I fit in to this, Mr McIntyre? What has that got to do with me, please? If you need to unburden yourself, I will mention it to the nurses and they will get the social worker to come in directly."

James Philpott was starting to become irritated.

"No, I don't need a social worker. It's you that I need to see. I too have been having an affair for the past two years- with your wife, Mr Philpott."

James looked intently into Douglas McIntyre's eyes. He waited for him to make another preposterous comment. He was used to dealing with patients who had delirium. This was no shock at all to him. Of all the ridiculous things the man might have come out with, this was so very silly. The man was playing out his fantasies. The accident had awakened ideas in his head that were purely fiction, just crazy notions after a serious car accident and brain surgery. The general rule was that the patient often blamed someone for the accident. This was somewhat of a new line, but the thread was the same. So his wife was singly to blame for the crash so she had to be vilified, for she was the one responsible. They had only met the couple socially together on one occasion. Celia loved him and no other. James Philpott knew that McIntyre's alcohol level had been measured after the accident and it had been a shocking 2gm. He would have blurred memories of the events before the crash even without that amount of alcohol in his bloodstream. He was looking at a suspended sentence for this, and a whole lot of aggravation from the Education service. It could possibly mean even a sacking. Celia would more than likely be involved in the decision making on that. This fellow's sub-conscious is working overtime to find a way out of the mine of trouble he is in, thought James. The actual words that McIntyre had uttered to James Philpott had had no effect at all upon him. The idea was ridiculous, too ridiculous for words and the doctor dismissed it totally.

There was no further word from the man in the bed. To an observer of the situation, James had taken in the information and digested it slowly, but the mere observer would now find it hard to analyse the surgeon's reaction, for there was none. He took the remarks as a professional would and shelved them in that file in his brain marked: nonsense.

He was irritated too that McIntyre had dragged him down here and wasted not only his time but also the nurse's. Par for the course, he thought. Without further ado, he excused himself to McIntyre, who kept on talking as he was leaving the room, raising his voice at one point, shouting that it was all true. Philpott left the room and called in at the nurse's station, making a note of the delirium he had witnessed on the patient's notes. He made sure to have a quick word with Nurse Whalley about what had been said. She looked totally embarrassed and started to apologise for having wasted his time. James Philpott smiled down at her and told her not to worry.

"All in a day's work!" he said, "and my day is over now. Good evening to you. I am going home and I can't wait. It's been a long day!" he said, smiling broadly into the young nurse's eyes and making her just a trifle embarrassed at the snippet of personal information he had just shared with her.

Now he could go home, he could tell Celia that the local headteacher had delirium; at least he knew that she would find it hilarious. Maybe the Head had fantasies about Celia; he could see why. But as he got to his car, he hesitated, wondering whether he should test the water first, rather than be jolly and talk shop, which was something he never, ever did. Things were not right with Celia; all he wanted was for her to be like she had been up until Saturday evening. Saturday...McIntyre was brought in on Saturday. Absurd to try and find a link between the two, he thought as he started the car. But there was no telling what was waiting for him there after Celia's recent conduct. It wasn't the right time to tell her what the headteacher of the school had been ranting on to him about either.

He would suggest a meal out tonight which might bring Celia out of this awful mood she was in. Not for one second did James Philpott try to connect the two things: his wife's strange behaviour and his patient's "delirium". They do say that the last person to know is the person closest.

Without another thought he rang Celia. The phone rang out and went onto to her lovely answer phone message.

"Hello darling, when you pick this up, can you ring me back, please? I'm just leaving the hospital."

Celia never rang back. She hadn't picked up the message yet, thought James as he drove the twenty-odd miles back home from the hospital. James arrived with a decision: to ask Celia to try and tell him what was worrying her. He had avoided the issue for the last three or four days, and he really felt that there was nothing that could not be resolved between them, theirs was a strong marriage, he loved his wife and he knew she loved him.

He opened the door and called out that he was home. This was his usual entrance, and when Fergus was there he would come running downstairs, desperate to tell his father how his football practice had gone or how he had managed to solve the latest riddle on one of his computer games. Fergus wasn't there of course so the house felt strangely quiet. They had been looking forward to his going away on the Scout Camp so much. The week was over tomorrow and nothing had turned out quite like he had expected.

James went into the kitchen, Celia was usually in there, but the kitchen was empty, no smell of cooking to welcome him either. James knew she was there because he had pulled his car into the garage next to hers.

He called out but there was no reply. Maybe she was lying down, he thought. He waited for a few minutes, pouring himself a drink. But he didn't sit down to drink as he would normally have done. He placed the glass on the unset table and was quite suddenly filled with fear, heart racing and head pounding. He leapt up the stairs three at a time and flung open their bedroom door.

Celia lay there, foetal-like. James threw himself onto the bed and shook her, willing her to wake. There was no mistaking a coma. Celia's eyes were closed, her pupils when he prised open her eyes were dilated and unmoving; her breathing was irregular. There was no response in her limbs to the pinching he tried immediately. James made all these checks in a few seconds, then immediately called the emergency services. He looked around the room, saw the upturned bottle of tablets and an empty half-bottle of brandy. The tablets were hers, sleeping tablets the GP had prescribed for her.

James knew that time was of the essence; he had given his name and occupation when he had phoned the paramedics and stated that it was a category A medical emergency. He was all too aware that swift action was needed, not only to save his wife's life, but to preserve her brain function. He phoned through to the hospital telling them what instructions he had given to the crew.

All this had taken a matter of two or three minutes, there was little more he could do. He knew the average waiting time for Category A emergencies was around 6 to 8 minutes. He carried Celia downstairs and laid her on the sofa, checking her pulse and heart rate, which were both irregular. He ran to the door, leaving it ajar, then ran back to her and started CPR. The phone began to ring, and finally the answer phone clicked on; it was Fergus, chattering on, saying he had tried Mum's mobile... James let the boy continue talking. It was almost more than he could bear. Time ticked on, an endlessness which was soon interrupted by the cacophony of sirens coming nearer along the road.

He was propelled into the ambulance. These men had no idea who he was and there was no point telling them. The wailing from that vehicle would pursue him forever. It was a sound so familiar to him yet so foreign now. He had never for one second thought of the pain people felt when their loved ones were being transported. He had been in on the receiving end in A&E for many years as an intern, then as a registrar. Yet he didn't really understand a thing about people and their pain, their emotions. His had been an easy life up until this very day. He sat in the ambulance crushed, desperate to help his wife, yet unable to do so. This was his worst nightmare. His own life would never be the same again, as he sat there cradling Celia's head in his hands, the life slowly ebbing out of her, his own life in shreds beside her. And then there was Fergus.

Anthony spent an hour or so in his room in Cambridge trying to organise himself a flight to Fuerteventura. He could get there tomorrow, which was Friday, but he would have to change his flight back to Singapore. That wasn't an issue for him, but given the situation with Lydia he really wondered if it were fair of him to consider going off to the Canaries simply because he wanted to see his father. That could wait, he decided, he had to help his sister, which meant cancelling his flight home to Singapore and giving her some support here. He would ring Laurence and arrange to see him.

*

We went out into Cambridge for dinner that night and chatted on about our respective lives. Finally the subject touched on Mother and he was clear and firm as he spoke,

"Mother needs to be put in the picture, but first things first. We'll go together to see Boswell in the morning and then ring Mother before turning up to see her."

The following morning we met for breakfast.

"Anthony, these are my immediate plans. I am going to get back into landscape architecture. I've decided that I will try and contact my old boss. I've no idea if he still works for the company where I was, but I'll find him and send off my CV. I'll be seeing a solicitor as soon as possible to set a divorce in motion. I am going to leave the apartment and rent somewhere for a time."

"I will lend you the money to set up somewhere, Lids," offered Anthony.

"Thanks, Anthony, but no; you see I know that I can still use the joint accounts. On an immediate basis, I plan to empty them all and open an account in my own name. I've found share certificates for tens of thousands of pounds in the safe. Many of them are in my name anyway. There is more money than I need. And I will get a job, I am sure of that. I am certain too that Douglas was mixed up in this murder and I want it cleared up. I want to move on now."

We went together to the police station where I made a formal statement. I could still not remember much about the incident but I could incriminate Douglas because of the keys and the phone. I told Boswell about the identity of the two people listed in the phone. He held up his hand to the person who was transcribing the interview, halted her, saying that this was "off the record",

"Mrs McIntyre, I am afraid there has been a development there and I think you should know this. Mrs Celia Philpott took an overdose yesterday. She is in hospital. We haven't had any more information than that."

I stopped short and gaped at the detective. I had rung her and then she had tried to commit suicide. There was nothing anyone could say. All our lives had been turned upside down by Douglas. When we came out of the police station, I told Anthony.

He held a hand to his mouth.

"You told me yesterday how you had phoned Celia Philpott and how the woman had been distraught. Didn't you say that the phone call had been cut short because Celia Philpott had hung up on you?"

"Yes, I was angry and hurt at what I had discovered. I don't want the woman to die though. At least no-one knows that I rang her".

We crossed over to the two cars. Anthony rang Mother. As she answered, I could hear her. Anthony skilfully led the conversation away from a confrontation; he arranged to meet her for lunch telling her that he would be staying a few more days. This somewhat defused the situation and caused Mother to actually thank him profusely.

We arrived rather earlier than expected at the hotel where he had arranged to meet Mother.

"I haven't told her that you are with me," he said.

"Then I am sure that it will be a lovely surprise for her."

Mother walked into the Punch Bowl Hotel dressed for lunch out with her son. When she saw me sitting with him, she was genuinely shocked. Before she had got an opportunity to say anything at all, Anthony broke in,

"Hello mother, sorry there has been a bit of subterfuge, quite necessary really, sit down, you need to listen to me, and without interrupting please."

She sat down dutifully, scowling at me.

"Lydia is leaving Douglas."

*

Jane opened her mouth and Anthony placed his finger over his lips, as one would to a small child in school. The gesture to silence her worked wonderfully well. He continued, telling her concisely about the crash, the events leading up to it, Douglas's involvement with Claire Leaver and Celia Philpott, his repeated physical and mental abuse of her daughter and his lies about their finances.

By the time he had got to the question of finance, Jane Waterman was looking around the room as if to escape. She was shattered. These two had no idea how she loved this man, no matter what they were saying he had done. She did not believe one word of it. It was evidently all Lydia's fault and now, to cap it all, the girl had invented a horrible story. Jane dared not voice her thoughts for Anthony was not in a mood to stand for any interruptions, she could tell. She sobbed quietly into her handkerchief, willing him to stop. She wished she were at the hospital now. They could say whatever they liked, none of it was true.

The waiter arrived to take their order and Anthony stood up with the menu and motioned the waiter away from the table. He ordered three club sandwiches then went to the bar to get Mother a double brandy. Anthony had not told Mother everything either. Celia Philpott's attempted suicide was for later.

D.I.Boswell observed the little red mobile phone that Lydia had left with him that morning. This wasn't an open and shut case at all. The results of the autopsy on Claire Leaver had come back; she was four months pregnant. According to the lease paper recovered in the flat Douglas McIntyre owned her apartment. She was paying him a nominal rent for it. He was a frequent visitor to the place; there were his fingerprints and hair all over the flat. Curiously, fewer traces on the balcony and hardly any at all in the bedroom.

When McIntyre had been formally interviewed, the interview had dealt mainly with his movements before the crash. Boswell had asked if he knew Claire Leaver but he had denied knowing her other than having said hello a few times to her as one neighbour to another. He wanted to know why there were all these questions about her. Boswell made a conscious decision not to tell him that she was dead. He skirted round the issue, feeling that McIntyre was in far too agitated a state to be told something like that. If he had killed her, he was acting as if his own accident had removed that part of his memory of events before it. If he hadn't killed her then he didn't need to know just then. Boswell went back to try and crack him but McIntyre had called for the nurse and said he was under too much stress, so the interview had been curtailed on medical grounds.

The detective had firmly established the man was the girl's landlord. He had installed her in the flat a few months earlier according to her diary entries. It was puzzling to D.I. Boswell who had questioned Mrs McIntyre about it. It was clear that she knew nothing. She had given him the bag of paperwork which she had recovered from the apartment and the safe. The search warrant for McIntyre's place had come through and the detectives were up there combing the place. Meanwhile Boswell was planning to re-interview the young jogger who had almost tripped over the body. As he was musing over all this, the door to his office opened and his young sergeant came in, a broad smile on his lips.

"Sir, we've just got back from the McIntyre apartment. Looks like we have solved the mystery of the link between McIntyre and the dead girl...we have found this passport application form in a drawer at the flat. He's put on it that he's her legal guardian."

"Right, I think we need to speak to Mr McIntyre once more and right away. Ring the hospital, will you? Arrange for me to do a full interview with the bloke, sooner rather than later. I'm not wasting any more time now that we have some concrete facts to throw at him. The man might not have told a total pack of lies, but he certainly hasn't revealed the truth either. If he's innocent, then he's in for a shock, and if he killed her then he's just added a lot longer to his sentence," said Boswell.

The interview was arranged for that afternoon. Boswell confronted McIntyre with the knowledge that his flat had been thoroughly searched and that they were in possession of clear evidence linking him to Claire Leaver.

"You knew Miss Leaver. "

"Yes, I've known Claire all her life. What do you mean "knew" her?"

"She's dead, Mr McIntyre. She was murdered last Saturday. The day you had the crash. "

Douglas's world came to an abrupt end at that moment. He adored Claire, totally worshipped the girl. He had been a student with her mother. Theirs had been an on off courtship and then she had got herself pregnant at a party and come weeping to him about her misfortune. She had refused to go for an abortion; the father denied everything, as one could in those freer days before DNA tests. During the pregnancy McIntyre stood by her, knowing the child couldn't be his but he did offer to marry the girl. He liked her, felt sorry for her. She had refused. She had brought Claire up on her own. McIntyre had often helped her out financially. He was the girl's godfather too. Her mother had died of cancer when Claire was at university. After that he had kept in closer touch with his godchild. When she had got that job in Cambridge, he offered her the use of the apartment he had just bought. The deep affection was all to do with her being part of his past, pre-Lydia,and he preferred it like that. Lydia was only five years older than Claire and it would have led to too many questions. He had told Claire that he didn't want Lydia to know what their connection was. Claire had tried to reason with him, telling him that she was bound to meet up with Lydia, so Douglas agreed to introduce them at a drinks party he planned to hold.

"We have nothing to hide, Douglas! It's not like we're lovers!" she had said on their last meeting, on that fateful Saturday.

This girl was not his lover, not his daughter, but a genuine link held them together. Douglas had been kind to her all her life. Her short life. And now she was gone. Boswell explained, as gently as he possibly could, what had happened to her. Douglas McIntyre laid in the bed and sobbed. Boswell stood patiently as he saw the man dissolve before him. He was not surprised. He had ceased to be surprised in his job. You just never knew what was going to turn up so you just got blasé. But he realised that Mrs McIntyre would not be expecting this. He was sure that she had had no idea that her husband even knew the girl before she tried that key in the lock.

Jack Lightson was the jogger who had found the body, had literally run into it. He was in the waiting room tapping his foot nervously on the radiator. He had already been in the interview room and they had got him down here again and were now holding him, pending "further enquiries." Jack had been trying to decide whether he should tell them everything. When they found out she was pregnant, then they would do tests and he would surely be implicated. DNA and all that.

Jack bent over and held his head; she was having an affair with that old man. He had seen him leaving the flat that lunchtime. He had watched him hugging her up above him in the stairwell and telling her everything would be all right. He had waited behind a pillar for a couple of minutes after McIntyre had roared out of the underground car park and then he had gone up to the flat. She had been surprised to see him, she thought he was in Cambridge. When he saw her there in that white dressing gown, with her hair all wet, he knew she had just been to bed with the old geezer and had got in the shower after he'd gone.

He had suspected something for a while. She was hiding something from him. And she'd told him that she didn't want an abortion. She was determined to go through with the pregnancy. She told him that her mother had done that with her and she wanted to give this child of his the same chances that she had had. He had shouted at her he wasn't even sure this baby was his. She had thrown her head back and laughed scornfully at him.

They started to argue and he pushed her in the lounge,

she screamed; he had squeezed her neck to keep her quiet, but then she just went limp in his arms. He carried her to the balcony and just lifted her into the air ... simple really. He just made it look like a suicide. And they would blame the old bloke. Jack had just slipped out of the building, then he'd run round the block and right into her on that pavement. He hadn't killed her at all, she had just fallen. It had been an accident.

Boswell came out of his office. Jack looked up at him.

"I have something important I need to tell you."

"Right this way, sir."

EIGHT

After three weeks in hospital, Douglas McIntyre was transferred to a rehabilitation centre. He had severe problems with mobility, lost his balance easily and suffered from chronic pain. Jane Waterman walked into the hospital the day after she had had that awful lunch with Anthony and Lydia; she told Douglas she would look after him until he could manage on his own. She hoped he would accept and he had. Jane was happy to have the man she loved on his terms, not hers. She had lost everyone else and she knew that she had to keep him.

Douglas was a broken man. Claire, his lovely Claire, was dead. Celia had been nothing to him but a diversion from work. He didn't care if he never saw her again. He secretly thought she had tried to kill herself because she had loved him. The idea appealed to him. As for Lydia, she had cheated on him too, he just knew it. Just like Jane Waterman, he too believed the stories that he had invented. After the rehab centre Douglas moved into a purpose-built flat in the town. He was dependent on carers. Jane came to see him often and took him out occasionally The education service retired him early, rather than sack him; that had saved his reputation to some degree but rumours spread around the little town until no-one was really sure what had happened on that day in April.

Celia Philpott recovered from the overdose, thanks to James's quick thinking. She waited and waited for James to confront her with the awful reality about her affair and her lies. So she was stunned when she found out that James did not believe Douglas's story. When he finally recounted the "absurd tale", as he called it, to her, she was recovering at her parents' home. She listened to him and remained silent. She had never fully appreciated her husband until that day. They never spoke again about it. James asked her if she would agree to leave the house, telling her he would really prefer to do that.

"It has too many memories for me, darling. I never want to walk into that bedroom with you again."

"Whatever you want, James," she said, knowing that he was right.

They drew a line under things with the move. Nothing was referred to again. She just knew that he was aware of the whole story, but there was a silent agreement never to bring it up again. So their lives rebooted when Celia left her parents' home. She never ever went back into the old house. James organised the removal and brought in a firm of people to pack up the place. One of the packers was surprised to see an iPhone tumble out of a washing-up bowl of stagnant water, but apart from that, the move happened without incident. James, Celia and Fergus moved into rented accommodation in a small village near Addenbrooke's.

Anthony came back again to the UK four months later to see Lydia. He was pleased that things had moved on considerably in her life. She had moved away from the town into a studio flat in Cambridge and the apartment was up for sale. The apartment was emptied and with it Lydia's life with Douglas. She told him that had gone along way towards sorting out the financial mess and was hoping for the divorce to come through before Christmas.

She had become much more important to him now. Strange how these few months had changed them both, brought them back together through all her troubles. He had come over from Singapore thinking that the two of them were going to Venice together as they had planned. He had really wanted Lydia to go with him but with her new work and appointments, she said that she didn't feel that she wanted that meeting just yet. She said that she was worried about rekindling a relationship with Father having just left behind so many emotional ties.

"I've had enough upheaval in my life for the moment, Anthony."

So he left alone for the exhibition, just as he had done in May when he had gone to Norway. He promised Lydia to come back and tell her all about his meeting before he went home to Singapore. He settled into the idea of seeing his father for the first time, just the two of them, and it made him smile. He took a flight from London to Milan and took the train to Venice. He had made doubly sure that Laurence was there, but had not let his father know that he was going. He had e-mailed him a week or so earlier and asked how he was, and how his work was going, and Laurence had written back sending him a link to his website with the forthcoming events.

The Venice exhibition was the next important venue and he was programmed to give a lecture in the largest Congress Centre at the Hilton hotel there. When Anthony booked into the hotel, he was impressed to see the posters about the exhibition around the place and people milling into the ballroom before the talk.

Anthony watched this kindly man, slightly stooping, walk on to the stage and acknowledge the clapping with a shy wave. He began talking and it was clear how much he loved his work and loved communicating that passion to people, more especially young people, for there were many many art students in the audience which numbered seven or eight hundred people. If he loved his work like that, surely he must love his children too?

Anthony listened intently to his father and was fascinated by him. He was proud to see how appreciated the man was in his field. He had the audience in the palm of his hand, he knew how to handle people. The conference drew to a close and Laurence announced that he would be willing to answer some questions. There was a local TV station filming and a couple of aides were in the aisles with roving microphones. Question after question came and Laurence was clearly enjoying the enthusiasm of his listeners.

"Mr Waterman, can you tell us when was your first exhibition and what were you exhibiting?

Laurence smiled and replied,

"It was many years ago, before you were born, I would think; I took my two young children to Deauville to the ceramics exhibition there. We went on the ferry and I had to put my exhibits in my son's pram."

Laughter from the audience. Laurence's present exhibits would have flattened any pram.

"Oh, I can see what you are thinking, but rest assured, they were only vases, asymmetrical designs on them, as I remember, looked delightful with tulips in them. Especially white ones. I carried my son for the whole weekend and pushed the pram and the vases to the exhibition in the Town Hall at Deauville. They didn't create much of a stir though, but arriving with them in a pram did! And my son is now 31, so that gives you an idea of how long ago it was. I just wish he were here right now to hear that!".

A platitude under normal circumstances, that throwaway comment at the end of his reply. Had his mother doctored the truth, or worse still, told a pack of horrible lies? As the thought came into his mind, the terrible feeling followed it that she had indeed lied, she had lied all the time, all through their growing up alone, without their father. He felt sickened. He didn't know if this hunch was right but he could now not dismiss it from his mind. He had to know. Anthony sat there and felt a wave of sadness sweep through his body. It was as if an imaginary veil had dropped from Anthony's eyes.

Further questions from the audience which went on for about ten more minutes. Anthony listened to his father and admired the man, looked at him as a man, not as his father. He studied his body language, looked at the creases on his forehead and around his eyes. Finally, Laurence held up his hand and said,

"Time for just one more question, now, otherwise I will be running over into the time allotted to your next speaker."

A host of people put up their hands.

"Yes, the gentleman in the pale blue sweater over here on my left, your question, please?"

The microphone moved across the hall.

"You said you wished your son were here to hear that story about carrying him on the ferry to Deauville. Dad, I am here, it's me, it's Anthony. I heard it."

The cameras were whirring. The TV crew was suddenly very active: their story of the conference now had a singularly human touch which would send the TV audience figures rocketing tonight. The editor of the programme was already starting to think of who he could sell the rights to.

The audience went quiet, and looked over at the man in the pale blue sweater on Laurence's left. There was an embarrassed silence and everyone looked towards the guest speaker and back to the man. Laurence leaned forward, squinted into the audience, moved forward. The arc lights were preventing him from seeing who had actually spoken. He was slowly taking in what had been said and somehow disbelieving, incredulous. By then, Anthony was walking down the centre aisle, people were standing and clapping, Laurence went right to the edge of the stage, Anthony vaulted through the orchestra seats and tried to pull himself up onto the stage. Laurence held out a hand to him and heaved him up and they embraced.

At that very same instant, Laurence remembered his fervent wish of many years before and he was smiling, joy filling his heart. He had waited a long, long time. He had been patient: my son, my own beloved son has grown up and today I am able to hold him in my arms and let him feel my tears on his cheeks. And Laurence could feel both their tears, for Anthony was sobbing too.

They turned to the audience, who were still applauding, and with arms around each other's shoulders, they each lifted up the other hand and waved to the crowd. It looked just like an election night scene. Many people in that audience were crying too. No-one knew why really, no-one knew the pain Laurence had been through, no-one knew that Jane had denied Anthony his father whilst he was growing up. No-one knew the joy they both had at finding one another again and not one single person in that whole place knew what Anthony felt in his heart at that moment: that they would never, ever be parted again; the time they had not had over the years was over. This was the start of their lives as father and son, lives which had been put on hold for such a long time.

They came off the stage still holding one another. It was as if they were afraid to let each other go. Laurence stood in front of Anthony and looked him up and down, up and down, peered into his eyes, asked him to turn around, took Anthony's hands in his and held them up to his face. And they embraced again, laughing and crying, talking both at the same time. Anthony could not get over the likeness they both had, the same hair and hands, the same laugh lines, the same height and above all, the same feelings of love one for the other.

They were just preparing to leave the wings behind the stage, when a young man came up to them.

"I'm Umberto Celli, reporter for Rai Uno, could you just spare us a moment? You see, we filmed your meeting and we'd really like some background on it."

"No story, please!" said Laurence, "this is just as it seems, a father and son and a surprise meeting, no more, no less."

The reporter pressed them but both of the men refused to be drawn; Anthony was suddenly a little worried. It had been a spur of the moment thing, he had not thought about the TV cameras, nor the audience, the only thing on his mind was the joy he had at seeing his father and the need he felt to hold him in his arms. He had not thought of the consequences.

They had so much to say to each other. Anthony suggested that they went back to Laurence's hotel and they took a taxi there. Once in the room, the phone started ringing. Newspaper reporters, the TV company, so that finally Anthony asked his father if he should book another room in another hotel. They did just that, but as they emerged from Laurence's hotel, they were surrounded by photographers. The only way was to go back into the hotel and stay in the room. Anthony spoke gently to the reception and asked them to block any calls.

Laurence looked worried and said,

"But I must ring home, they will be worrying about me. I ring once a day, just to let them know I'm fine."

Anthony said, "Please, Dad, don't worry, this will all blow over and by this time tomorrow, we'll be out of here, away from Venice. You can phone now from your room or you can borrow mine if you like," and handed him his own phone.

They went back to Laurence's room and sat there together, talking. Question after question, the questions coming mainly from Laurence; Anthony felt some kind of embarrassment at asking his father about his present life, he didn't want to know about his father's lover or her son. He had heard about it from his mother and felt it was Laurence's business. Laurence wanted to know what Anthony had studied at university, where he had worked, for whom and when, what he liked to eat, what books he was reading, whether he liked gardening. Did he prefer tea to coffee, no question was banal here. Neither of them touched on the people in their respective lives. It was as if there was some forbidden ground between them that neither dared tread upon. Nevertheless they had much to talk about, so the one person who linked them kept coming up time after time: Lydia.

Anthony talked a lot about her and told his father how she had turned her life around despite a situation which could have easily destroyed her both mentally and physically. Douglas had had a car accident in May. Anthony explained how he had come over for a week while Douglas was in intensive care. Whilst he was over in the UK, he had rung his father but when he had heard that he was in Norway, the idea had come to him to come and visit him there, and as he found that he could get a flight to Norway, he had booked a trip and visited Vigeland Sculpture Park and the Kongresscenter. Anthony explained that he had missed Laurence by a few hours.

Laurence listened to him and asked some questions about Douglas, but Anthony was unable to give all the answers. He knew Douglas had been in a critical condition at first but was recovering now. He then told his father about Lydia witnessing a horrific incident, a murder in fact, at her flat on the same day as the accident and her involvement with the police as a crucial witness.

"Poor girl, I am sure your mother will be trying to help her all she can."

Anthony realised as his father said that, that in fact he really meant it. The man had no ill feelings for his former wife or if he had he had buried them deep inside. The same could not be said for her. The two people could not be more different. Anthony gently explained that Lydia now saw nothing of their mother. He didn't elaborate on why and Laurence did not ask.

Anthony explained that he had come over again to see Lydia, but that he had planned the trip to coincide with his father's exhibition. He had been following his activities on the internet as well as keeping in closer touch with Lydia since Douglas's accident.

"Why didn't you let me know?" asked Laurence.

"To be honest, Dad ..."

Anthony stopped as he said that and hugged his father again.

"I just wanted to surprise you, I am sorry for all the wasted time, the wasted years."

Laurence was touched by his son's emotional outburst.

"It is such a pity Naseera and Hakim aren't with me, they were supposed to come but she is so busy at work at present and Hakim is doing well at school, he is at secondary school and he really didn't want to miss the start of the new school term. I made a promise in Oslo that I wouldn't do another trip without them but Naseera pleaded with me to come here. She is such a help with the business side of things."

Anthony looked down shyly as his father spoke of his life with them. Laurence sensed the embarrassment and put both his hands on Anthony's shoulders.

"Anthony, although you might find it odd, as everyone else seems to do, Naseera and I are not a couple, yet we aren't like father and daughter either. No-one could replace you or Lydia ... ever."

"But Mother told us that Naseera and her son ..."

Laurence stopped him.

"Hakim is her little brother, Anthony. Your mother has got it all wrong. She didn't know the story so she has woven her own version of events and it appears also considerably embroidered them too. To tell you the whole truth, my life was lonely and empty for many years and then one day, about six years back, when an exhibition took me to Tunis, I was able to return with not one, but two rays of sunshine. The two of them are responsible for my recent happiness. I have no hold over either Naseera or Hakim but we do live as a family. I am neither father to them nor am I a lover to Naseera. All I am is a happy member of a loving family that I chose and more importantly, who chose me. I have been able to help them and they have given me what I needed and craved for all those barren years – affection, company, a reason to carry on living. But they did not, and never will, replace you. I left you and Lydia when your mother threw me out and I never let one day go by without mourning that."

Anthony was in mute admiration of his father. Even though he knew that Jane had told them lies, Laurence preferred to let them believe her rather than upset them and have to involve himself in their life with their mother. Anthony respected his father even more than before. This was a truly great man, an altruist to the core, he thought. He was angry at his mother's shallowness and bitterness. She had chosen to alienate both him and Lydia from Laurence.

"She shouldn't have made things up, she could have just said she didn't know, which would have been the absolute truth."

"Your mother probably sincerely believes her version of events, Anthony. You cannot alter that. She will not have told you maliciously. Nothing I have ever done in my life has ever pleased your mother. I am now able to look back on our brief lives together as happy, because I did exactly what your mother wanted. The day I refused to do so in order to follow my way as an artist was the day your mother showed me the door. Of course she never expected me to walk out of it, but I did. And I have never looked back, Anthony. True, I lost you both, but the alternative was to have your mother create mayhem over custody and visiting rights. I just was too weak to stand all that. No one puts the children first in these cases. The adults just want to make sure that the children continue to love them when they live apart from each other. It is guilt which drives the adults not love. It's the adults who cause the disruption."

"She told us you had cut the whole family off and that you never paid any alimony. She told us she had struggled to pay us through university and college."

"Anthony, she had her reasons, it is largely irrelevant. You are who you are and you still love me, no matter whether I paid or I didn't. Don't harbour grudges, look where it has got your mother. Tell you what, son, after I have rung the family in Fuerteventura, let's give the girl I love most in the world a ring, shall we? Let me speak to your sister."

*

I put the phone down and smiled. At last I was moving forward and it didn't feel strange; it felt right. Those years which had been filled with moments of fear and foreboding were at an end. Years brimming with unsaid words dissolved before me. I had wasted much time, so from this second onwards, I would relish every moment and enjoy life, savour what time I had. I was only 35 after all. There was a lot to think of. I no longer had to put up with acid remarks I had been used to from Mother throughout my teenage years and all during my ill-fated marriage to Douglas. I had taken it all from both him and Mother and never once retaliated. Perhaps I was like Father as she had so often disparagingly told me. I was healing slowly. There were decisions to be made and I was alone now to make them. Life had moved on around me for so many years. I had walked away from Douglas in that hospital over three months ago and had not looked over my shoulder once.

The first decision had been simple. The police had requisitioned the apartment and I had handed over the keys without a second thought. Before I had left the area I visited a solicitor, who had checked out all the finances. Douglas had put many of the assets he had in my name to avoid tax. The upstairs flat was even in my name. The joint assets were being looked at and his sole assets were under scrutiny too. I had filed for divorce citing mental cruelty and had asked for half of the joint assets. All of my belongings amounted to three suitcases. It seemed a terrible situation to the rest of my contemporaries but I was so happy. I had moved into a studio flat in Cambridge. Anthony had again insisted on sending me the first year's rent, telling me in a note that he wanted me to have some breathing space before making a move that I might regret.

Neither of us have made any contact with Mother; I have not seen her since the day I walked out of the hospital. There were a few shrieking phone messages, then a few more contrite ones but after a couple of months they ceased. I soon realized that life before that day in the hospital only contained acquaintances, people who were ships that passed in my marriage. Both were over. I knew that I would become an after-dinner subject at Bridge Club, Golf Club, Rotary dinners and meetings.

James and Celia Philpott have left the area too, but I have no idea where they have gone to. That's part of my life I am glad to forget. I am just grateful that she recovered from the overdose; on reflection, I don't wish her any ill luck at all.

Somewhere I heard someone say one day, "You need to learn to cut out the dead wood in your life". My mental pruning shears have certainly done that. I make no attempt to contact those ships from the past and no-one gets in touch with me; I know why. I didn't mean anything to anyone. I just existed at Douglas's side. Dead wood indeed.

I quickly settled into a routine in Cambridge; nothing was so enormously different to my life before. I performed all the same tasks, prepared the same kind of food, shopped for the same kind of products, but there was one change - everything was for me and me alone. I bought myself a new wardrobe, changed my hairstyle and splashed out on a new computer with a state of the art landscaping programme.

Then I began to make plans. I realized that I needed to get back to my former career, not for money, but to prove to myself that I could do it. There was still a cloud of sadness and self-doubt clinging to me. It was still hard for me to accept that so much had happened. There was no doubt in my mind that I had gained rather than lost, yet there was a nagging thought that I was now alone; no-one to ask me questions or to have to answer to. The relief that I felt at first began to leave me and as the past faded into memory, I realised that the present and the future was all up to me. I refused to let myself dwell on the lonely aspect of my life. My life was mine to do with as I wished after all. Before long an idea began to form in my mind. I contacted my old boss, and asked him for advice. He had also left the company where we had worked. He was now in London running a French architectural company. He invited me there to talk over my re-entry into the employment market.

"You made a good impression on me when we worked together. You can count on me to help you out to get back into some work. I'll put your name forward for a post here. I don't want to lose you to a rival!"

"Thanks, but no thanks. What I need is your advice and I'd like you to listen whilst I outline some plans. You see, I have decided to set up my own company, working with garden designers to landscape existing properties. The idea isn't new. I thought things through when I was at the old place, but then ... then I left the job. I know that by combining my ideas for contour and design and their skills with choosing the right trees, bushes, plants and flowers I could ..."

I told him all about my idea and showed him some plans I had drawn up using derelict sites with properties remaining on them. Nicholas Wade was speechless. He realised that the quiet, unassuming girl he had worked alongside ten years before had blossomed. There seemed no reason why she needed to take such a risk because work for someone of her calibre was forthcoming.

"So you feel that you want to go into running a set-up yourself rather than working for someone else."

"Exactly that."

I looked at him carefully. I had never taken a risk before but yet strangely, I had no longer any fear of making an error. Nicholas Wade was more than enthusiastic and gave me lots of advice all of which was positive. He put me in touch with several garden designers whom he had met on other projects and invited me to the next Chelsea Flower Show as a consultant. I knew that if I had the project up and running by May when the Flower Show was held, then I had every chance of coming into contact with people who would be interested in my work. There was absolutely no doubt in my mind that my project would be successful. I would not, I could not, fail.

There is a huge difference between the Lydia I was a few months ago and the Lydia I am today. I have been catapulted into the true adult world. Even my time working as a landscape architect had not given me the impetus to assert myself and forge my own way forward. Now, today, this very second, I know that I have enormous talent and that talent is going to burgeon. I am standing on the balcony of the office restaurant and thinking back to a previous moment on a balcony, staring out, not knowing how to move forward other than to try and snuff out the life in the being who crushed me relentlessly. How foolish and cowardly that seems to me now.

The tomorrows I have to look forward to now will never see me dwelling on those of my past. The door to that former life is firmly bolted.

From the meeting with Nicholas Wade, I went to see an agency who specialized in setting up small companies and laid out my project. The person I saw was enthusiastic when I told her that she could phone Nicholas Wade. He gave me unconditional backing. We organized a further set of meetings for the following month with a view to having the company running by early February. I began to make enquiries about premises. Nicholas had put me in touch with a couple of garden designers and one of them phoned me the week after my trip up to London.

"James Monks here, yes I got your number from Nicholas, I might be interested in working with you. My projects are in need of expert advice and he has recommended you very highly. Could we meet up to discuss things?"

"Certainly", I said. I was positive that I could make a success of this new venture. After all, I was on the brink of a new beginning.

Anthony came back from Venice elated. He took me out to dinner.

"Lids, I really want you to make plans to visit me in Singapore. If I give you the dates, will you fix it up? You see, Father, Naseera and Hakim are coming for Christmas. You can't be busy for that date."

"Yes, Anthony, I'll come."

I will go and meet my Father and celebrate a true family Christmas for the first time in many many years. And it will be worth waiting for.

*

Eighteen months after that fateful Saturday, Jack Lightson was finally convicted of the manslaughter of his pregnant girlfriend, Claire Leaver. Douglas and Lydia were both called as witnesses. They crossed one another in the court building with blank stares. By the time the trial took place, the former Mrs McIntyre was a divorcee, running a successful business with premises in Cambridge. Her father and brother both came to the UK to support her through the trial.

The prosecution was convincing in arguing that Lightson had premeditated the killing. The fact that he had tried to implicate the dead woman's landlord went heavily against him. His defence argued that he had committed the crime in a moment of anger and the jury went with that theory; after all, he had confessed to the crime in Boswell's office on that day in April a year and a half before and he had shown considerable remorse. He had been on suicide watch whilst on remand. He was found guilty and given a fifteen year sentence.

Three years have passed since then. The crash, Claire Leaver's murder and all those dark days are fading into the past for those who were involved. Looking out over the bay, there is another head-scarfed woman who too is lost in reverie. She's gazing way beyond the North Sea as she walks along the empty promenade. The pretty garden blooms once more with those swaying daffodils and hyacinths. On that promenade in the east of England on another balmy day in April, Jane Waterman stops. She has learned to live with an annual visit from Anthony. After all he is so very busy. She is glad that that cheating daughter of hers is out of her life. She looks towards the beach and sees the waves curling over the sand, disappearing fast into it. She sighs as she leans over to adjust the tartan blanket which is catching a little in the spokes of the wheelchair.

About the Author

MAGGIE M. GRIMSHAW spent her childhood in Darwen, Lancashire. She went to teacher training college in Leeds, West Yorkshire, majoring in French. Her first post was in Huddersfield, West Yorkshire in 1976 at Almondbury High School, then at Wellhouse Middle School in nearby Mirfield. In 1986 she moved permanently to France, setting up her own business as an interpreter, translator, tutor and teaching assistant in primary schools. In 1995, aged 42, she passed the national French Civil Service exams and taught English at high school level in SW France for 18 years, working also as lecturer in education at Toulouse University and advisor to newly-qualified English teachers. She has participated in the production of several text books and CDs for the French educational market. She retired in June 2013.

Surf over Sand is her first novel. In the summer of 2012 her husband searched out the manuscript, thinking it was completed and had 50 copies of it printed as a surprise birthday gift for her. Maggie gave them as presents for Christmas 2012 and with the very good reviews she received, she was prompted to finish the book. She also intends to write a sequel to the story and has plans to write a third book about a life full of surprises in La Belle France. The French version of *Surf over Sand* will be coming out in 2015.

Lightning Source UK Ltd.
Milton Keynes UK
UKOW03f0734020414

229275UK00002B/130/P